HUMAN WORLD

HUMAN WORLD

Daniel Amedee

Boyle
&
Dalton

Book Design & Production
Columbus Publishing Lab
www.ColumbusPublishingLab.com

Original cover artwork by Michael Protzik
Copyright © 2019 by Daniel Amedee
LCCN: 2019931993

Paperback ISBN: 978-1-63337-251-1
E-book ISBN: 978-1-63337-252-8

Printed in the United States of America
1 3 5 7 9 10 8 6 4 2

PROLOGUE

SHAN

A pulsing blue light cuts through all that is. One second everything is there and the next everything isn't.

I open my eyes in a place I've never been before.

White walls made of rock. Granite. Limestone. Onyx. Quartz. Diamond. Stone. And the taste of copper in the back of my throat.

Giant cliffs that reach up into a white haze. The sound of water. This is not where I was before. This is not land I have ever seen. I haven't seen land since the floods.

But the others are here with me. My group. Mok, Z, Ped, U.A., Morla, Pata. And me. Shan. I am Shan.

I wanted them to be here with me. I asked them here.

This was all arranged. We all knew!

But… No… We didn't. Something else did. Something that isn't me anymore. Something primal. Something bigger.

We agreed to meet here now! We agreed.

What cruel joke of death is this? Put me here in a… What? A cave? On a beach beside the ocean? Surrounded by cliffs? With people I've never met? What do you expect of me?!

Shan. I am Shan. Mok is here. I know it's him. He's the soldier. Still in his brown radiation suit so no skin will be exposed in the battles for the land. I should tell him he can take his helmet off. No need for it here.

And Z. She's here in her patchwork clothes same as me. Common attire for the ships. She looks peaceful. I don't think she's woken up yet. I guess no one has.

And this one. Ped. I don't remember much about him. He isn't from Earth. Or is he? Orange shirt and pants? It's not possible.

Pata will be a problem. He doesn't want us to know he was on the moon. But he shouldn't try to hide it. It doesn't matter now.

And U.A., the woman from the underground huddled close to Morla, a daughter of the ships. The privileged woman in yellow and the hazel-eyed girl in rags. They both look like they want to be so tough but they're so innocent.

But who am I to talk? What do I have to offer these people? Why do I feel like it's my responsibility to offer anything?

The thoughts of a moment. Soon I will feel compelled to speak… Once the shock wears off. We'll all start to speak.

And I am afraid of what we will say.

I

SHAN

It's incredibly easy to become disillusioned. Some would say it's our natural state and we have to work very hard not to be.

I agree.

We are all disillusioned and reality has become a byproduct of mental disorder.

There are no exceptions.

• • •

Shan: "Is everyone OK?"

I look over the group. I don't have anything to offer, so words will have to do.

Z: "I think so."

Ped: "Yes. Thank you."

Mok looks at me and nods.

They are the only ones to respond. The others are still too shocked to speak. Too stunned to make sense of it.

Morla and U.A. sit in the fetal position, shoulder to shoulder. Pata lies curled up on his side. Mok, Z, and Ped sit next to each other with their backs against the white cliffs. They're looking straight ahead at the white cliffs in front of them. And the white cliffs to the left. And the white cliffs to the right.

I sit and run my hand through the rocks and stone and mud on the ground. All white.

The water sounds so close. Like there should be an entrance to this walled-off alcove and on the other side will be the ocean. But we are surrounded by white cliffs rising into a white fog as high as any of us can see.

It's not a big place. It would only take a minute to walk the perimeter. But it feels like we are surrounded by a vast emptiness. By a peacefulness. By the calm before the storm.

There is a truth in the stillness. But I don't know how to find it.

I live with foreboding that nothing can stay peaceful forever. Eventually the tide rolls in and it's swim or drown. Eventually I have to live.

What good am I if I sit in my tower above the rest of the world in enlightenment and let all that's below sink into the sea?

What good am I with the knowledge of the universe if I can't be a part of the world?

How disillusioned I must be.

2

PED

I never believed in much of anything. But that doesn't mean I didn't want to.

Most of the time I believed in ideas about greater powers and how they applied to the self and to the whole. Pseudo-spiritual beliefs about God or a higher power. A collective consciousness that we were all a part of.

I believed we were destined for a golden age, or that nirvana was at our fingertips if we only just allowed it to be.

I would meditate and contemplate and trick my mind into going places I thought were real. Different planes of existence, higher states of consciousness, worlds beyond the physical, but it only existed in my imagination.

It helps us to believe in something, but in the end it just becomes violent. People start to believe they have the one right answer and they know what's right for everyone else. It's better when we don't believe in anything and just let it all be.

But it's not in our nature to give up control.

• • •

MOK • Z • PED • SHAN • U.A. • PATA • MORLA

Z slowly gets up and walks over to U.A. and Morla. U.A.'s yellow clothes radiate in contrast to the white of the place. Morla looks like a rag doll next to her. Z puts her hand on Morla's shoulder and sits down next to them.

She looks at Morla the way only a mother can.

Z: "What's the last thing you remember?"

Morla looks back at Z with big eyes.

Morla: "I was on the ship… In the cafeteria… There was a long line to get food, longer than usual. There weren't any clean trays. Which was odd… They always seemed to have so many trays…

"I eventually got food. Bean protein or something like that. It was all the same. The food from the labs…

"I sat down with a group of friends and just stared at my food. They asked if I was OK. I said something like "yes" or "I don't know."

"I could feel something wasn't right but had no way to explain it. They didn't press me about it… We all had our bad days.

"Then everything started to vibrate. I looked around to see who else felt it. I think they did. They looked scared… Confused…

"Then the shock wave, then the pop, then…"

Z: "You were here with us?"

Morla: "Yeah."

• • •

MOK

We were all hungry for different things and we made ourselves believe whatever we needed so we could feed. We ate whatever life force got in our way.

Clawing on the backs of others to rise to the top just so we could feel special and in control for however long this lifetime would grant us this egomaniacal dream before cutting us down. Timeless story.

We had all earned a right to be here. I had earned a right to be here. I know that. But how? Why?

Am I supposed to be some sort of leader? What good was I to anyone when I was alive? Am I still alive?

I take off my helmet, set it on the ground beside me, and look over the group.

Do these people rely on me?

No. They can't.

3

MOK · Z · PED · SHAN · U.A. · PATA · MORLA

Z thinks she's helping Morla feel better but she's really just trying to make herself feel better.

Z: "None of us really know what's happening."

Morla: "Yeah…"

U.A.: "Is that supposed to make her feel better?"

U.A. wraps her arms around Morla and pulls her in close, rubbing her shoulders.

Z: "Maybe…"

Morla: "Don't do that."

U.A.: "Don't do what?"

Morla: "Make things harder by acting like this. She's just trying to talk to me."

A tense moment of silence is broken by Pata's voice.

Pata: "What about me?"

Everyone looks at Pata lying on the ground, curled up on his left side, slowly rocking himself back and forth. No one had realized he was awake. Or hadn't thought about him being awake or asleep. No one had thought about him.

Mok is the first to speak.

Mok: "What about you?"

Pata rolls up from his side and looks at Mok.

Pata: "Are none of you interested in how we got here?"

Pata scans the group. Hostile. Angry.

Shan looks up from his study of the rocks and stones.

Shan: "Do you know how we got here?"

Pata's gaze quickly falls on Shan and for a tense moment they just stare at each other. Pata's eyes fall away.

Pata: "No…"

• • •

PED

I ignored the truths that stared me right in the face.

I chose to believe stories based on… What? Faith? Fear?

I saw the world thrive on chaos.

I've never seen people happier than when everything is wrong.

We all have to feel alive some kind of way. I helped create that world. There was a part of me that wanted it that way.

Is that how we ended up in this place?

• • •

MOK • Z • PED • SHAN • U.A. • PATA • MORLA

Mok: "Eventually we have to do something…"

Morla: "Maybe before long we'll all start to get desperate enough and just give in…"

Everyone looks at Morla in silence. No one wants to ask the next question.

U.A.: "Give in to what, Morla?"

Morla looks up at U.A., who still has her arm around her. Looks right into her eyes. Big, sad eyes. Eyes that give away what doesn't want to be said. U.A. instinctively rubs Morla's shoulders and looks away.

U.A.: "We should wait until we have more information."

Pata: "And where is that supposed to come from?"

Silence.

U.A.: "I don't know…"

Pata: "How many times has help just appeared?"

Mok: "Eventually we have to do something…"

Shan: "But what are we supposed to do…?"

Shan runs his hands through the white rocks and stones and mud. The others stare at the cliffs.

4

MOK

A group of people started petitioning to change the name of Earth to Ocean.

They said Earth was a misrepresentation.

I had no arguments for or against. I think the majority were past the point of caring, and the time when people had enough energy to argue over semantics was long past.

When the invasion began... Well... You become something you never thought you'd become when the only option you have is to follow your instincts to survive or die. When you're forced into the present moment, you don't have time to think or rationalize. You just do what needs to be done and maybe you'll be able to cope with it all later. Or maybe not.

The relief of truth is profound if you don't get crushed under the weight of it.

• • •

PED

We're dependent on the stories we tell ourselves. The stories that start out rooted in some truth that gets misinterpreted and convoluted over time. The stories that become myths.

We lack the depth to understand the truth buried in them. But we cling to them with desperation.

The myths of how the Earth came to be…the remnants of catastrophe…the signs of a greatness that once was…

Even when the past rises out of the depths and all the pieces fall into place, we still have a hard time accepting any of it as true. It's just easier not to.

We lost our way over time. Let the stories become myths. Let our history become fiction. But we can't run from it forever.

• • •

MOK • Z • PED • SHAN • U.A. • PATA • MORIA

Sit and think. Sit and think. The only thing any of us can do is sit and think.

The only sound to focus on is the steady pulse of an unseen ocean. The only sight to see are the white cliffs surrounding us.

What is this place?

Pata breaks the silence.

Pata: "Well?"

U.A.: "Well what?"

Pata: "What are we supposed to do?"

U.A.: "You can't really expect any of us to know that…?"

Pata: "Someone has to be the expert."

U.A.: "Why can't it be you?"

Pata: "Good luck with that."

Shan: "Enough, you two."

Silence.

We look to one another and at the white world that surrounds us.

5

SHAN

I always told myself *one day at a time*. All the events of the world will unfold around me and the best thing I can do is try to keep up to speed with myself. And with my family. And with my work.

Try to raise my children to be sane in a world of fiber-optic implants and nerve stimulation and virtual reality plug-ins and blood motors and…

This was before we had to move onto the ships. Before life became straightforward. Before we were forced back to a simpler way of life.

Then I told myself this war was the best thing that could have happened to us. It was violent and chaotic but it snapped us out of the daze we were in.

Sometimes change can only come when…

A soft pop pulls me back to the white cliffs, and a line of blue light starts to grow out of…

What? Nothing? Out of the stone? From crystals in the rock? From the charge in the air?

An electric line of static blue grows in the stillness of our white prison and electrifies the air around us.

I stand up and walk over to it. Slowly. The others rise and follow behind.

Shan: "I've never seen anything like this before."

Z: "I don't suppose any of us have."

We all move closer. We form a small semicircle around this blue crack forming in front of us out of nothing.

Ped: "Touch it."

Ped bumps Mok with his shoulder.

Mok: "No way."

Ped: "Draw straws?"

Mok: "Do we have straws?"

U.A. has her arm around Morla, holding her close. Morla had tried to inch away and get closer. U.A. needs her more.

All eyes turn to me.

I look at them. Uneasy.

Shan: "OK…"

I slowly move my hand closer to its surface, and I get hit by a wall of energy that pulls my mind in a swirl up and up.

I am lifted out of my body…

I see things I don't understand… Atoms and particles… Time and space… Astral and causal…

As quick as the visions come, they go, and I'm slapped back with the others.

Where are we?

When I open my eyes I'm lying on my back and the group stands over me.

Morla: "What happened?"

I look at their faces. They all look different… But… How? Their faces all look like different versions of the same face… Like they are all the same but different somehow…

They slowly shift back to the faces I know… But…

Shan: "I don't know…"

U.A.: "Is it safe?"

I look at U.A. She looks afraid. But so do the others.

Shan: "I don't know how to answer that question."

Pata: "You have to give us something."

My eyes turn to Pata as I start to roll on my side to sit up.

Shan: "Well… See for yourself."

• • •

SHAN

The world is both flat and round. It all depends on where you're standing.

Frequencies make planes. Planes make matter. Matter interprets itself through cognitive functions. Cognitive functions create space and time.

Out of what has no substance comes a world of substance. Flat and round.

MOK · Z · PED · SHAN · U.A. · PATA · MORLA

Pata walks slowly to the growing blue crack and reaches out his hand. The second he touches it he falls to the ground like all the life has been taken out of his body in an instant.

He starts shaking and curls up into a ball on his side. He starts muttering and then screaming. It looks like he's having a seizure. The white rock and stone scratch against each other as he shakes and screams.

Pata: "What was that? What was THAT?! WHAT WAS THAT?!"

We hurry over and Z kneels down to comfort him. She rubs his back and tries to get his attention.

Z: "Calm down! It's OK! Pata! Look at me! It's OK!"

We all stare down at the shaking mass of Pata.

The relief is profound if you don't get crushed under the weight of it.

Is this what Pata was meant to be? Is this the real man? Is this what he becomes when put face-to-face with reality? The real truth?

We have to keep telling ourselves we're here for a reason.

This group… We know each other. We know we know each other… We know we've talked before… But…

Then Morla shouts.

Morla: "Get ahold of yourself!"

We all look at her in shock. Pata stops shaking and looks up at Morla in fear. Whimpering. Z sits him up.

Morla stands by the growing blue line and glares at Pata like she would if she were scolding a puppy.

Pata's voice trembles when he speaks.

Pata: "You touch it and see if you're telling yourself the same thing."

U.A.: "It's OK, Pata. Everything's fine."

Pata: "How can you say everything's fine?"

Morla: "What does it matter either way?"

Pata: "You've got to be kidding me!"

Z: "Just sit. Think for a second. Let yourself catch up with whatever it was."

Silence. We all stare off in thought. Some look at the ground. Some at the cliffs. Some at the blue crack in space.

But Morla stares straight at Pata, her back to the growing blue. Larger than all of us but just a child.

After a while, Shan speaks.

Shan: "Everyone should take a turn. Touch it. See for yourself."

Pata: "No!"

Shan: "It's the only option I can see."

Pata: "Well, you're not looking hard enough."

Morla: "You're looking too hard."

Pata: "Just stop!"

Morla sticks out her hand and disappears into the blue.

• • •

MOK

People had to start living on boats. Repurposed cruise ships mostly.

The wars for the land seemed like they would never end. They grew more hostile every day, consuming every last inch of available mass. People had no choice but to start living on the water.

The continually rising sea level didn't help much either.

They say something happens to your brain when you're put in a position of power. Even those with the best intentions lose empathy and their pineal gland calcifies.

You see no repercussions for your actions and you think you're perfectly right in destroying the lives of millions for your own gain.

I agree.

But then what does it mean to be human, anyway?

• • •

PED

There's so much love in people. I have to remind myself of that.

The kinship... The embrace...

Even through the negative, the love people need and give is staggering.

How could we have forgotten that? What was it that made us detach from it?

It baffles me.

7

PED

People stopped being interested in knowledge. Knowledge was no longer power. Ignorance was power. And people started to equate ignorance with happiness.

And those with wisdom were so used to being on the sideline they just removed themselves from the game altogether.

I assume we'll be fine... We're all fine. We've always been fine. It's our perception of the world that isn't fine.

We put too much pressure on ourselves anyway.

But that's what life is, isn't it? Waves of good and bad... A fake happiness is much worse than a real sorrow.

I never trusted being happy.

• • •

MOK • Z • PED • SHAN • U.A. • PATA • MORLA

Before we can process or react to Morla being gone, she's back. We are frozen in awe.

There she is, standing exactly where she had disappeared only moments before.

Z: "I don't understand…"

Shan: "I'm not sure we're supposed to."

Z: "But…"

Z stands up and walks over to Morla. Z looks wary but not afraid.

Z: "How?"

She slowly circles her, looking for something. Anything. She hopes to find the truth in this girl.

Z: "How did you do it?"

Morla looks shocked. The brave girl who stuck her hand into the blue isn't the girl who came back. She looks fragile. Her eyes are a deeper shade of hazel.

Morla: "Your guess is as good as mine."

Z: "Where did you go, Morla?"

Morla looks at Shan. Her voice shakes a little.

Morla: "There's a man coming for you. He seems very nice. Very kind. He's coming to help."

Shan: "What are you talking about? What man? Where did you go?"

Morla: "I saw him by the ocean. It won't be long. He's coming for Shan."

Silence. We all look at each other, unable to make anything of what she said. Words so simple and so foreign.

Shan: "Who is coming? And what do they want with me? By what ocean?"

Morla: "He was wearing a blue robe. His hair was all white. It all happened so fast. I'm sorry."

Morla walks over to U.A. and buries her head on her shoulder. They both sit down and U.A. wraps her arms around Morla and rocks her back and forth.

Everyone stares off in silence until Mok speaks.

Mok: "So now what?"

More silence. More helpless stares at the infinite white. More trying to make sense of the senseless. Simple minds trying to comprehend the incomprehensible.

Then the world starts to get brighter.

Shan breaks the silence.

Shan: "I can feel something moving."

We can all feel it. The blue crack in the world starts to get bigger and brighter. It starts to hiss and snap. Little bolts of electric blue move in darts through the air.

Something is happening to Shan. It's happening to all of us, but it only feels like a distant memory of what Shan is living.

Shan: "You don't feel that?"

A wave of energy rolls out from the blue toward Shan.

He starts to gag.

We all try to move toward him but we can't move. A wave of nausea rolls through each of us.

It feels like there's another body inside of Shan that isn't his. It's being ripped out. It's being ripped out of all of us.

Shan collapses onto the white rock and stone.

8

SHAN

A being shrouded in white light, wearing blue, stands next to me. On a cliff above the ocean…? On a platform…? Is that sand…?

It looks like the ocean, but I've never seen water like this before. It's as if millions of crystals are bending light, shining from below.

"It's good to see you again."

Shan: "What do you mean? Who are you?"

The platform drops out from under me and I fall feetfirst into the ocean.

• • •

PED

I had always believed humans were not made for Earth. Just look at our inability to coexist. With nature, with animals, with ourselves, with anything…

We had separated ourselves as a society from all the things that would align us with a peaceful coexistence with the world around us. And without our intellect we would have gone extinct so quickly we would have been the laughingstock of evolution.

Or maybe it was our intellect that got us into this mess, and evolution is looking down, doubled over in laughter.

But I never believed much in evolution. We were put here. And left here. A half-assed test-tube baby created by a race so advanced we decided to call them gods. And they didn't even want us.

• • •

SHAN

A hand slaps my face. Softly and repeatedly.

Z: "Hey! Hey! Are you OK?"

My eyes slowly start to open and the group stands over me. Z has her face close to mine as she taps the side of my cheek.

I don't feel the same anymore. I can't explain what I mean by that.

Shan: "I think so…"

Morla: "What happened?"

I look around the group and try to remember what happened.

Shan: "I'm open to suggestions."

Z: "You just passed out."

The group backs away a little and I sit up on my elbows.

Shan: "Did you see anything?"

Z: "What…?"

Shan: "Did anything come out of me?"

The group shares quick glances back and forth.

They must think I'm crazy. But why would they think I'm crazy? Those rules don't apply here.

Morla: "What do you mean?"

Shan: "Did you see anything come out of me?"

Z: "No…? Are you feeling OK?"

I dig my hands into the white rocks, the stone and mud.

• • •

PED

Of course humans were meant to be on Earth. If not, then why?

It all depends on what you focus on. Your perception. Your state of consciousness.

There is peace and harmony. And there is chaos and discord. One cannot exist without the other.

I have to keep telling myself that.

9

SHAN

I know these people. I know I know these people.

But the more I think about it… How?

I've never seen them before… I don't have any conscious memory from my life that involves any of them. I didn't live with them on the ship. I didn't work with them in the labs before the invasion.

So why do I know them? Why do I feel so comfortable around them? Like old family. Like someone you haven't spoken to in years, but right when you see them you pick up where you left off.

I walk over to Morla. She sits next to Z against the cliff and stares up at the white.

Shan: "You saw him too?"

Morla: "That man?"

Shan: "Yes… He was right there next to me… Standing on the ledge before it gave way… You said you saw him when you disappeared…"

Morla: "Yes. I saw him."

We just look at each other. We each expect the other to have the answer.

Z: "Are you feeling OK…?"

I look at Z.

Shan: "I don't know how to answer that…"

• • •

PED

There will always be some trivial thing we miss from our previous lives. Something that we'll over-fantasize… As if having that one thing will bring it all back.

We dwell in our imaginations and our beliefs on the way things are meant to be without giving much merit to the importance of the way things are.

As if things wouldn't be this way if they weren't meant to be.

• • •

SHAN

It's obvious the subtle movements of this place are starting to have an effect on all of us. It doesn't feel like we are in danger. But it doesn't feel like we're safe either.

It is starting to feel like we're extensions of one another. When one of us gets a leg cramp we all feel our muscles twitch as it gets massaged out.

When one of us thinks something it appears as a new idea in all of our heads.

When the white of this place blends into tones and different textures of all the different shades of white, we can't tell whose eyes we are looking through... Our own...? Or one eye that shows us all the same thing...?

It feels like we are supposed to be here. Like it's natural.

But how...?

10

z

Everyone's bank accounts were frozen and seized for "emergency funds." To fund the war effort. We were well into life on the ships by that point and no one was really working in the modern sense anymore anyway. But we were still allowed to move what money we had around —"invest" in whatever war bond was advertised on the ships. Gamble. Pay for odd jobs or a bit of luxury. The people who had money on the ships tried to use it as a way to feel superior.

Grasping at straws…

Once that was gone those people drifted further and further away. No one was more special than anyone else anymore. Some people couldn't handle that.

But most of us didn't care either way. I didn't care either way. It was just another thing that didn't matter anymore.

I had my daughter and my little community at sea. I had a life that, after a time, made more sense than the one I had been living on land.

Before long, all communications stopped. It was a relief to be free from the propaganda.

We were on our own. Left to survive or die on our ships. That was life. Just like it had always been. Just a new take on an old theme.

• • •

MOK · Z · PED · SHAN · U.A. · PATA · MORLA

The sound of the waves grows louder. From a faint sound of a soft crashing on shore to a riotous roar of a tempest battering against rock.

We all turn to look at the blue line as it starts to crack the air with pops of electricity. With waves of energy coming from somewhere beyond our white prison.

The blue line grows. It looks like it's reaching out toward Shan.

We can all feel him get tense as he loses sight of the group. A blackness pulses around the edges of our vision as Shan slips into darkness… Why won't this thing leave him alone?

Should we feel grateful? Is this how we discover the truth of this place? Of what happened? But why Shan?

Shan starts to lose consciousness... The weight of the pressure building in his head is too much... It's too much for all of us.

The wave of energy pushes its way up from the bases of our skulls and Shan disappears...

• • •

SHAN

I am running through a forest at full speed.

Where am I going...? Am I being chased...? How did I get here...? Why am I running...? Why...?

The dirt is soft and gives easily under my feet. I dig in with each step, and the feeling of earth between my toes makes me smile.

I can run forever. I can't help but laugh!

The joy of running! On solid ground! I haven't felt real ground in so long!

And then I see them. I freeze in place and stare.

There is a group of four...monks?...standing in the distance at the edge of a clearing beyond the trees. They have on pale blue robes and their faces are...shapes. An oval. A sphere. A triangle with rounded edges. A cube. I can't make out their features.

They are standing on the outskirts of a village. They turn and motion for me to follow.

I pull myself together and walk slowly to their tiny settlement.

MOK · Z · PED · U.A. · PATA · MORIA

Shan is just gone. We don't know what to do so we all just sit there and look at each other, or at the white cliffs, or the white sky, or the growing blue crack in space.

Z moves over to sit next to Mok.

Z: "Where were you before this?"

Mok glances at Z and then away.

Mok: "I don't think it's important."

The others move closer to Mok and Z, eager to talk about something. To take their minds off it all. Or to try to put it all together. Or to just not feel…whatever this place makes you feel.

Z: "It could be… I'd like to know."

Mok: "Wherever we are now is a lot better."

Silence. We don't want to press him. But…

Z: "It's just… We never heard anything about the war… Just rumors… And propaganda. And then after a while, nothing… We were just left on our own…"

Mok: "I had a lot of different orders… Basic stuff mostly… Shoot and kill… My most recent orders were to claim land and make it safe enough for a terraforming ship. A giant converted aircraft carrier with gardens and all kinds of plants and whatever."

Z: "What happened?"

Mok looks up at Z, smiles softly, and looks down with sadness in his eyes.

Mok: "The ship got bombed. We had managed to keep it hidden for a long time. It wasn't the only one, but it was the main one…"

We are all silent for a long while.

Pata surprises us by breaking the silence.

Pata: "What was the war like?"

Mok: "I don't know… It's just the way life was."

• • •

MOK

Really it all started when the moon cracked open and what was inside came out.

The private aerospace companies loaded up what ships they had ready and left for good, going to other planets they hoped would accommodate refugees. From what I heard, most tried to make it to Venus. We didn't even know Venus was inhabitable. It didn't make any sense.

But people flocked to the spaceports with the hope of making it off Earth. Desperate for anything. There was no real criteria for who got to go. You were just in the right place or not. They either had enough room on the ship for you or they didn't.

It all happened so fast… The invasion…the running…the hiding…the surviving…the evacuating…the terror and the drive and the thrill of it all!

It became obvious the governments weren't interested in resolving any of the growing issues with the people, weren't interested in being of help to anyone but themselves. When no one could pretend help was ever going to come from our leaders, then private companies took it upon themselves to do what they could. It was ironic.

All the cruise ships were converted to renewable energy. Some had solar panels. Others had water turbines. And they were outfitted with food labs and water filtration systems and reworked to accommodate as many people as possible.

It all happened so fast...

The governments went underground. There were cave systems and bases and farms and subdivisions all connected by high-speed trains or transportation platforms.

The invaders from the moon used an electromagnetic weapon that sent out a vibrational field that separated the atoms of the physical body.

Physical life vibrates within a certain range of frequencies, and at a specific rate that makes matter appear solid. These electromagnetic weapons accelerated the physical frequencies, forcing them to no longer exist in the physical spectrum. People would start to vibrate and scatter apart and just disappear.

The moon people would set off massive electro-magnetic pulse bombs near the entrances of underground bunkers to break apart the energy seals on the bunker doors.

Massive amounts of electrical energy would get released into the atmosphere. Slowly, over time, the energy built up. I think that's how the blue light came to be.

• • •

MOK • Z • PED • U.A. • PATA • MORLA

Z reaches out her hand and touches the white cliff. It's soft and smooth, almost no bumps on it. In some places it's clear, and a whole range of colors bouncing off of each other extends as far back as the eye can see. Layers of colors move in the rock.

Z walks over to Mok. He sits there and stares at the blue crack.

Z: "Are you feeling OK?"

Mok: "Yeah…"

Z sits down next to him.

Z: "What's been happening to you?"

Mok: "I'm not sure. Have you seen anything? Felt anything?"

Z leans her back against the rock.

Z: "Little things. Waves of different colored light. Particles of… something. I hear something like a high and low pitch bouncing off one another. When I close my eyes I can see lines of light vibrating in a grid."

Mok: "Have you talked to any of the others about it?"

Z: "Not really."

Silence for a moment. Z can feel Mok think.

Mok: "I don't know how to say this."

Z: "Do the best you can."

Mok looks to the ground and then over at the others and then over at the growing blue crack.

Mok: "I saw that same blue crack just before they set off the last electric bomb. It was like…"

Mok pauses.

Z: "What?"

He takes a deep breath.

Mok: "A detonation had never looked like that before."

Z: "What do you mean?"

Mok: "It was like something had shifted the energy. Like it was being captured and diverted, like the energy from the bomb was being collected and redistributed throughout the entire universe… It was massive. I saw a blue crack start to grow in the sky… And then…"

Z: "Pop."

12

MOK

You either made it on the ships, made it off-planet, or you were left behind. Some said those left behind were the lucky ones, but...

No one really wanted to be left behind. That would mean wanting to give up. To just lay down and die.

I didn't want that. So the only chance I had of survival was to join one of the infantry battalions.

I think most people would have rather died.

• • •

MOK · Z · PED · U.A. · PATA · MORIA

U.A.: "Where were you?"

U.A. sits close to Morla on the ground. Morla stacks the white rocks and stones and knocks them over and stacks them again.

Morla: "Somewhere in the Pacific… At least that's what they told me. I was born on the ship. So it was all just water to me…"

Z looks over to Morla.

Z: "My daughter was born on the ship too. She was probably a little older than you… Her father died just before we made it on the ship. I didn't even know I was pregnant then…"

Morla looks at Z with big, sad eyes. The thought of tears is there. Sorrow. Sympathy.

Morla: "I'm sorry. That must have been hard."

Z: "It was… But we all did what we had to do."

There's a short silence. Morla turns her attention back to U.A.

Morla: "Where were you?"

U.A.: "I was living in one of the underground communities."

Mok raises his head and looks at U.A.

Mok: "How?"

U.A. looks at Mok quickly and then away. She's embarrassed to talk about it, but she knows it doesn't matter. She knows she can talk about it.

U.A.: "My family had a connection with one of the heads of Nautico. It was a little personal village she had built. Under the radar. The governments never would have let us if they knew…"

Mok never takes his eyes off U.A.

Mok: "Nautico."

U.A. meets Mok's eyes.

U.A.: "Everyone wanted to do something. They were in a position to do something big. To get all the companies together to convert the ships. Build shelters. They saved a lot of people."

Mok: "Not nearly enough."

Silence. We all look from U.A. to Mok to U.A. again.

U.A.: "You're right. It's never enough. But at least it was something."

• • •

SHAN

A group of children plays in a river next to the small settlement.

I am sitting on the grass next to the riverbank when I feel a hand on my shoulder. I look up and see a monk from the village standing over me.

Its face is an odd shape. It's the shape of a human but longer and more round, like an oval.

The monk speaks to me but its mouth doesn't move. Does it have a mouth?

"You can come inside now."

I get up and follow the monk into a tiny wooden hut. The four I saw earlier are sitting on the ground in a line. They motion in unison for me to sit. Together they raise their right arms, and slowly light starts to shine from their palms.

The world gets brighter and I am alone in a white void.

13

MOK

I had to rethink my definition of human.

In the past if someone did something awful you'd ask, "Are they even human?!"

After a while, humans were the only living things we knew of left on the planet.

So what did that mean?

We were living in a human world, but it didn't feel like there was anything human about it.

• • •

SHAN

I stand on a disc-shaped platform in the middle of... What?

White space. Infinite white space.

But...?

There is a blue line in the distance. Almost like the horizon. But it's moving. Like a distant shoreline...

Waves start to bleed out. Dark blue bleeds into pure white.

I can't see where it starts anymore...

And then nothing.

I am back with the others.

• • •

MOK • Z • PED • SHAN • U.A. • PATA • MORLA

And just like that, Shan is back, standing there next to the blue crack in space.

He falters from the weight of his body on his legs and stumbles over to the white cliff to lean on it.

We all hurry over to him.

Morla: "You're back!"

Z: "How are you feeling?"

Z reaches out and rubs his back.

Shan: "OK."

Z: "Just OK?"

Shan breathes heavily. He does his best to stay on his feet.

Shan: "It's hard to explain… How is everyone doing?"

He looks around at all of us and then down at the white rock and stone.

Z: "It's all affecting us in different ways…"

Ped: "We're still not really sure what's going on, but… When I close my eyes I'm in a garden. It's still hazy, not solid. I'm here but I'm also there and there's someone there with me, but… I don't know."

Silence for a moment. No one knows what else to say.

Shan: "Right… And everyone is being affected?"

Everyone glances around at each other.

Z: "Yes, in different ways, but nothing like you… We've all been here…"

Ped: "What's happening to you…?"

Shan looks at Ped.

Shan: "Well… Let me sit down and I'll start from the beginning…"

• • •

MOK

We learned about the human cloning that had been going on for decades. We learned that most of our "leaders" had been grown in incubators, raised on military bases and trained from awakening how to be the perfect soldier, the perfect senator, the perfect president…

No wonder they didn't care about real people. They were created to be self-serving egomaniacs for what was ultimately a war machine.

Empathy was bred out. The only way to rule is to rule without emotion! Never let your personal feelings affect the bottom line!

For some reason these things were perceived as righteous. The next step in evolution or something… But when catastrophe hit they couldn't conceive of the world as a whole being more important than their own survival.

They were just puppets anyway.

• • •

MOK • Z • PED • SHAN • U.A. • PATA • MORIA

After Shan tells us what happened we all sit and stare at the white cliffs, or play with the white rock and stone, or walk the perimeter of our white-cliff prison, or lie down and close our eyes to try and make sense of everything.

When that gets old we huddle around each other for comfort.

Mok breaks the silence. He has something on his mind.

Mok: "They started breeding people without pores."

Ped looks the most concerned out of all of us.

Ped: "What do you mean?"

Mok: "It was a way to reduce chemicals leeching into the body."

Ped: "Oh my god…"

We all focus now on what Mok has to say.

Mok: "Soldiers wouldn't succumb to microbiological attacks or get polluted by the toxins being released into the atmosphere during the battles. The only thing they needed to protect was the face…"

There is a long pause.

Mok: "Without pores the body would obviously start to overheat… So they started making them cold-blooded…"

14

PED

There's a wealth of information buried in our subconscious.

So many beliefs…sorrows…disappointments…buried truths we don't believe in yet…

How could anyone be expected to find treasure buried fifty feet down off the coast of an island off the coast of a country off the coast of a continent that hasn't been discovered yet?

I guess there's always blind luck.

• • •

Z

People started jumping off the ships. Angry and embittered. Lost in the face of hopelessness. Seeing that as their only way out. Even after having come so far… And having been so lucky just to get on…

It was normal, almost expected, for there to be a few deaths every month or so. But when it grew to four or five a week we knew we needed to do something…

But where had knowing we needed to do something ever gotten us?

The ships started out as overcrowded and chaotic places. Masses of people just trying to make sense of the days and years leading up to this present moment.

Eventually it all settled down and the people who were on the ships felt like they were meant to be there. Like the test was over and those who couldn't cut it were gone. So they were allowed to breathe easy.

The people who were left settled into a routine. Some could say they even found a version of happiness.

• • •

MOK • Z • PED • SHAN • U.A. • PATA • MORLA

After Mok's story we all need to focus on something different. Z turns to U.A.

Z: "Tell me about the underground village."

U.A. looks up at Z like she is being pulled out of a dream and back into reality. It takes a moment for her eyes to focus on the group.

U.A.: "It was nice. We had everything we needed. We couldn't go outside but we had simulated sunrise and sunset. The ambient temperature rose and fell with what a typical day in spring would have been. In general we just lived."

A brief pause.

Z: "Did you have any contact with the outside world?"

U.A. takes a deep breath in. Exhales.

U.A.: "No… Not really. Every now and then an alarm would sound and we would go into small sub-bunkers. We were far down so the odds of them finding us were low, but it was good to be safe."

Ped joins the conversation.

Ped: "Then what?"

U.A.: "What do you mean?"

Ped: "Do you remember getting here?"

There is a pause as U.A. looks vacantly at the white stone and rock.

U.A.: "It was strange. I just remember feeling odd. A foreboding… Do you know the feeling you get before someone shouts? Or there's a loud noise? Almost like you're being prepared for something, or reacting to it before it happens?"

Ped: "I think so…"

U.A.: "Well it was like that. I was sitting on a bench in a park at the center of our bunker, then everything flashed blue and I was here."

15

PED

Bodies in motion and in pain and in joy and in rest.

We all take the steps we need to take. We set aside what we can't carry and shrug off what we can't take on. We have to keep moving.

We migrate through time, hoping to find comfort in a moment. We never fully heal or mourn. We have to protect ourselves if we want to survive.

We carry all of our past with us. We let it create our future lifetimes in flesh and bone. Our sorrow becomes encoded in our DNA. It becomes a blueprint for future generations.

We are layers upon layers upon layers of experiences and lifetimes buried inside a flesh suit.

• • •

MOK • Z • PED • SHAN • U.A. • PATA • MORLA

Shan has started to walk to the perimeter of our cage, softly count-ing each step and touching the surface of the white cliffs as he goes. Sixty steps to make the circle. Then he pauses, looks into the white rock, and starts over from one.

U.A. and Morla play with white rock and stone. They dig into the ground and build little figures out of the white mud.

Pata lies on his side, curled up. He rocks back and forth. He hasn't been right since he first touched the blue.

Mok, Ped, and Z sit together and watch while quietly talking.

Ped: "Do you think we'll ever get out of this place?"

Mok: "It feels like we will eventually."

There is a pause as Z looks at Mok.

Z: "I'm sorry you had to go through that…"

Mok: "Go through what?"

Z: "The war. The fighting. All of it."

Mok: "It's OK. I'm sorry you had to go through it too."

Z: "Yeah."

There is silence as they sit and watch the others.

Mok looks to Ped.

Mok: "What about you?"

Ped looks at Mok and then away.

Ped: "It's the strangest thing."

Z: "What?"

Ped: "I left Earth. We had gotten off."

Z: "But… Then why? How are you here?"

Ped: "I don't know."

• • •

MOK

It slowly started to come out that humans had landed on Mars and Venus and Saturn and had spent years on the moon, developing colonies and relationships with the locals and sharing technologies.

They had learned an original race of humans had populated these planets hundreds of thousands of years ago and had ultimately abandoned our ancestors on Earth. We were all the same race, we had just evolved on different planets.

The air force also disclosed they had time travel technology, and had for decades.

Apparently they did what they could to try and stop it, but in the end… The ones who knew, and cared, tried to make people understand the danger we were all in. But the warnings fell on deaf ears.

And since the time travel technology had been given to us by the people of the moon, our travelers had a different viewpoint on what they were seeing. They had come to the same realizations about the future we're coming to now.

They were shown where we had come from and where we were going. They were shown the reasons behind why it all had to be this way.

Most of the time travelers wanted all of this to happen. And knew it was better for all of us if it did.

· · ·

SHAN

The blue line has grown.

And it keeps growing. In smalls bursts and pops.

It affects all of us.

I feel like I can find a way out of here. Find a crack in the cliff wall. Find some kind of doorway to the water on the other side. If that is water I hear on the other side.

If I could see above the white haze… If I could see the top of these cliffs, then maybe… Maybe I could climb them…

And then Pata speaks.

Pata: "I don't know how much longer I can pretend it's not here. This awful crack in the world…"

We all look at him. He is sitting up and looking at the growing blue line.

Shan: "I don't think we should be…"

I walk closer to the blue. This is our way out.

Isn't it?

I just don't want to think about it. Pata's right. How long can I pretend it isn't here? Like it isn't the answer to all our questions.

It's like the others know what I am thinking.

Mok: "You might as well…"

Ped: "Do you really think that's a good idea?"

Shan: "Do you have a better idea?"

Z: "We'll be waiting for you to get back."

Pata: "If he comes back."

Shan: "I'll come back."

I walk closer to the growing blue.

I know if I hesitate…

I reach out my arm and it pulls me in.

16

z

When I first made it onto my ship I felt like I couldn't get clean. Like there was no way I could keep up with scrubbing off the toxins my body was pushing out through my pores.

My husband had just died and my body was starting to tell me I was pregnant. Everything that land had done to me was oozing out.

I had a void in my gut from losing my husband that was being filled with a life I was terrified of being responsible for... That I felt guilty for bringing into this world... What kind of a life would this baby have? What world was I even trying to sustain by continuing this cycle of birth and death?

I felt like I was using so much water that the filtration wouldn't be able to keep up. Like it would take all the oceans to get me clean.

The filter systems were designed to pump water out of the oceans, clean it, and store it in giant tanks. When any amount of water was used the system would refill it. There was never a chance we'd run out.

But there was never a chance I'd get clean either.

• • •

SHAN

I'm in an office… There are filing cabinets, Rolodexes.

A man sits at a desk. Is it the same man from the platform over the sea?

No.

Older.

He is filing reports. Millions and millions of reports. Reports that flow into the deepest parts of the past and into the furthest reaches of the future.

He looks over at me and hands me a folder.

"Here you go."

Shan: "Thank you."

"The reading area is just over there."

There is a small group discussing something quietly. Several others are deep in contemplation over the files in front of them.

I sit down at the nearest desk and open the folder.

It's filled with pictures.

Ancient people. Modern people. Animals. Beings I have never seen before. Life-forms completely unfamiliar.

In one picture a tribe dances around a fire.

In another, a group of people have dinner together.

A family goes on vacation.

There is a group living in a bunk system on one of the ships.

In another photo there is a group huddled around a fire in a torn-up city.

There is war and peace. Technologies I have never seen.

Some things I am familiar with. Some things eat away at me. Some things I can't bear to look at. Others I feel a longing for.

There is one image that catches my attention in particular.

I am smelting iron into gold inside a pyramid made of copper, mercury, and stone.

· · ·

MOK · Z · PED · U.A. · PATA · MORLA

We all look at the growing blue as it creates a fissure in this world. We all look at the space Shan was standing in a moment ago.

Morla breaks the silence.

Morla: "Do you think he'll come back?"

We all keep staring at the blue.

Z: "I don't know what to tell you…"

Morla: "I know…"

There is silence. We all want to say something… But what?

U.A. picks up a white stone and rubs it between her hands. She looks at it closer and sees it's more than just white. It has colors moving in it. Colors she didn't know existed before she saw them in this rock.

U.A. watches as the colors slowly pulse outward, forming a small grid around the rock.

U.A.: "It's the strangest thing."

We all turn our attention to U.A.

U.A.: "I remember this. All of us being here. Together."

Ped responds.

Ped: "I don't think that's strange."

U.A. looks up at Ped.

U.A.: "You too?"

Ped: "Yes."

17

PED

Culture wasn't really a thing anymore. I never understood why our leaders never saw the need for art.

The drive to be an individual was eaten up by the ego's drive to have more money than everyone else. You were a hero if you had the biggest bank account. Our world didn't leave any room for artistic expression. We were all too busy working to eat and to have a place to live.

We were flesh machines locked in a world of distortion, all following a life path in a system we were born into with no hope to change anything.

What culture grows out of a society driven by financial gain? What value does a human life have when it can't pay enough to be valuable?

• • •

MOK • Z • PED • U.A. • PATA • MORIA

Pata hasn't moved in a while. He just lies there, rocking himself back and forth. We start to worry. But he knows we are starting to worry, so we all think it's just a matter of time.

Z turns her attention to Ped.

Z: "Tell us more about where you were."

Ped: "I'm not sure I can…"

Z: "Try."

There is a pause.

Ped: "I had gotten on one of the transport rockets leaving Earth, an AeroTec one… I had heard about it, packed up what little I had, and started making my way there with my mother and father. It was a shot in the dark. I didn't really know what we'd find or if we'd make it… But what else were we supposed to do?"

Z: "What was it like?"

Ped takes another moment to find the words.

Ped: "Crowded… Not a lot of room to move but we made it on. People weren't used to space travel so a lot of people got sick… Some died. My mom and dad… It was hard."

Z: "I'm so sorry…"

Ped: "It's all right… I can't complain… I knew I had it better than most… We all lost someone… At least we were—"

Ped is cut off by a loud pop. Tension grows in the air around us. The blue crack sends out a pulsing signal that beats into our chests. The energy builds.

Mok: "What the hell is going on?"

Pata looks up at the crack as it widens in front of us and then he quickly looks away. He quickens the pace of his rocking back and forth.

Pata: "Shit… Shit… Shit…"

The blue starts to grow and spread.

A form starts to appear.

• • •

Z

The ships started to come together in different regions around the oceans to form larger communities. We would travel in small circles, moving out from a center point, trying to make contact with anyone in the area.

Every so often, contact would be made with a military vessel. A strict voice would shout over the broadcast channel saying we were nearing hostile waters or something like that.

We'd back off. Follow orders. No one was looking to join the fight.

18

MOK

Major riots had started on the land. People got tired of being herded around like cattle. You couldn't blame them.

People started guerrilla factions to fight the governments. To try and rise up and take some of the power back.

But the governments knew everything. Where the major faction leaders were hiding. Where weapons were being stored. Where they got the weapons. Where the biggest resistance camps were.

Everyone thought they were being so careful.

Once they found a cell it didn't take more than a couple hours to kill them all off. And before long there weren't any left.

It wasn't long after that when the majority of the population was moved to the ships.

• • •

MOK · Z · PED · U.A. · PATA · MORLA

Slowly a shape starts to form out of the blue.

Morla moves closer. She walks up to the being slowly but without fear. She speaks.

Morla: "Is it you…?"

U.A.: "Is it who?"

Morla looks back at U.A.

Morla: "The man I saw…"

The entity appears fully in front of us.

We don't feel threatened. We feel… Calm?

There's silence as we observe each other.

He's tall and full in build. He wears a light blue robe. White hair and a beard cut short and dark brown eyes.

But it's hard to see clearly. There's an energy around him that makes everything hazy. Like he puts off his own light.

We all stare. Unable to form words. Frozen. Waiting for something…

Then he speaks.

"I am here for you. My job is to study your world. Keep it in order. Monitor the shifts. See the byproducts of decisions. Your world is not destroyed. Be calm. Know each other. You have everything you need here and now."

19

MOK

One of the major companies that helped was Nautico. They started as a cruise ship manufacturer for luxury cruise lines, but became one of the only chances any of us had for survival.

They pulled together other companies to build something sustainable. They combined all the resources they could to build something for their fellow humans...so our race could survive.

They were praised as heroes. And rightly so.

• • •

MOK · Z · PED · U.A. · PATA · MORIA

The entity raises his right hand and starts to dissipate.

We all continue to stare at this being… Lost in awe… Filled with more questions than answers.

He shifts his gaze to Morla.

Z notices first.

Z: "Your skin…"

Morla: "What?"

A light starts to shine outward from Morla. A slow glowing pulse coming from deep within.

Z: "You're glowing red…"

Morla looks at her hands. At her arms. Touches her chest.

Morla: "How?"

Pata jumps up and rushes toward the being fading off into nothing.

Pata: "What are you doing to her?!"

He tries to grab the being, to pull him back into our reality.

Pata: "Stop it! Why are you doing that?!"

Pata grabs at nothing. The being isn't flesh and bone. He's not physical. He's made of light… Or of some kind of energy…

Then the entity speaks.

"Be calm. All is well."

Pata: "I don't believe you!"

Pata screams at the man. Desperate. Hopeless.

Z touches Morla on the shoulder and looks her in the eyes.

Z: "Can you feel that?"

Morla looks herself over.

Morla: "No…"

There is an acceleration in the air around us.

Morla's body begins to vibrate into electric lines. Waves of static moving in and out of existence.

She starts to break apart.

And then she's gone.

• • •

SHAN

I close the folder and walk back to the man at the desk.

He looks up at me as I hand him the folder.

"You're done already?"

Shan: "I think so…"

"People spend years here, poring over the pictures."

Shan: "Really?"

"You don't know where you are, do you?"

Shan: "No…"

"Amazing."

He puts the folder down and turns away, busying himself with his task once again.

Shan: "Where am I?"

No response.

Shan: "What is this place?"

The man at the desk says nothing. He just files and sorts as if I'm not there.

I turn and start to walk toward the door.

"Don't forget this."

I turn back and the man slides a small card across the desk. I pick up the card and see it has a thirty-three-digit number on it and nothing else.

Shan: "What is this?"

"A reference number."

Shan: "For what?"

No response.

I put the card in my pocket and walk to the door.

20

All life was a game. Filled with rules and regulations and guidelines. The struggle for money…for jobs…for happiness…for success…

For love. It was all so small.

What made anyone think any of it was so important? We hadn't created anything that was timeless or that would last any great stretch into the future.

All great societies in our history had collapsed and their technologies had been forgotten. And we hadn't made anything that could even compare to what had come before us.

Look how long it took us to figure out that the pyramids were hundreds of thousands of years old. Much less what they were meant for.

All we did was create new mythology and folklore and start the struggle to find the meaning of life all over again.

• • •

MOK

We learned the people from the moon and Venus were hybrid humans who had been there since The Great War was fought hundreds of thousands of years ago. They were a part of the original seed race for Earth.

We learned the moon was an old starship that had docked in orbit around the Earth. That the moon people had been studying our spiritual evolution as a species. Monitoring us. Guiding us as if we were their children.

The governments knew they were there. They were using the moon people to gain better technology. Apparently they thought the moon people were peaceful. That they only wanted to help.

They weren't wrong.

• • •

SHAN

I open the door to the office and step outside.

I find myself in a giant hallway. It looks like it stretches on for miles and miles. It's made out of marble and has giant columns that go up higher than I can see.

The marble is a sandy white and has veins of color pumping through it. The colors move through the stone like blood through our bodies.

I walk for a little while, passing doors, ladders, pathways leading to other corridors.

I stop in front of a door that looks to be made out of wood. Dark, dense wood. Old and solid. It has no handle or latch so I lean into it and it slowly starts to open.

When it opens enough to enter I find myself back in the office, where it appears that the same man is sitting at the same desk.

"How may I help you?"

I walk over and hand him my card.

"One moment please."

He disappears amid the stacks behind his desk.

I walk around the room and look over to the reading area.

This one is empty. Where are the people? Is this the same room?

"Here you go."

He hands me another folder that looks identical to the one before.

Shan: "What is this place?"

He looks at me and frowns slightly. Curious. He tilts his head subtly to the left.

"The hall of records."

Shan: "What is that?"

He stares at me in silence, and after what feels like an eternity he speaks.

"Reading area is over there."

• • •

MOK • Z • PED • U.A. • PATA

Pata curls up on the ground again at one end of our white cliff prison. But he isn't rocking anymore. He just stares. We don't know which is worse.

U.A. sits on her own. She gathers white rock and white stone and white mud together.

Mok, Z, and Ped sit next to each other at the opposite end and look at Pata. Then they look at U.A. Then at each other. Then up into the white haze. They look as the world around them slowly gets brighter and fuzzier.

Z breaks the silence.

Z: "Did you ever make it to one of the off-world colonies? After everyone left we really didn't hear anything else about the space-ships. Or the people on them."

Ped is pulled out of a dream. He was somewhere off in another world. He focuses himself back into the present moment.

Ped: "We did. It took about three years but we made it to Venus. It was way more than a colony. I had no idea. The city I was in was massive. Infrastructure and technology like I had never seen… The city was called Retz."

U.A. speaks up from where she sits.

U.A.: "What were the people like?"

Ped looks over to her.

Ped: "Fantastic. They looked human but their presence was more like what we longed to be…"

Z: "I wish I would have been able to see it."

Ped: "I think you may be able to soon…"

Z: "What do you mean?"

Ped: "Well… I've been trying to figure out why I'm here…

"I mean, the event you've all mentioned… I wasn't anywhere near it. I was on another planet…

"But I was in my small garden in front of my little refugee house and I remember getting very dizzy. I heard a pop right before I lost consciousness and then…

"Here I am…"

There is silence as Ped looks around at each of us.

Ped: "And that being, the one who just appeared here… I've seen him before on Venus…"

21

PED

How do you know all the secrets of creation haven't already been revealed? That it all isn't right in front of our faces? And the mind in its chaos and irrationality and noise just hasn't been able to see any of it?

We talk and we talk and we talk and we talk and we never take the time to listen. Like saying a bunch of things will make someone understand you. When you don't even understand yourself.

• • •

MOK

The governments realized too late that disclosure would have been a better idea than trying to keep people believing in the cover-up. I still don't know what they were trying to achieve. They had only made it more difficult for people to swallow the truth when it couldn't be denied anymore.

The moon detached from orbit and cloaked itself somewhere near Saturn. The soldiers from the moon were using some kind of teleportation time tunnel to get to Earth. It seemed like there was a never-ending supply of soldiers always appearing.

But when the moon was no longer there to lock in the tides, the water started to rise. Water from deep within the earth started to get pulled up and up and up, flooding the planet. It seemed like it would never stop.

• • •

SHAN

I sit down in the reading room and start to look through the pictures.

These are different. These are all pictures of places. Places I have never been before.

Except…?

One picture is of a stone monastery. Squat. Tough looking. Almost like a fortress.

Another looks like a large settlement built on a cliff on the side of a mountain. There isn't any way to get to it. No pathways or steps. The rock faces around it are too sheer.

Another building is a large dome and the sky around it is purple. There are massive columns carved out of what looks like marble.

There is another that looks like it's made of glass or crystal. Giant spiked peaks and rooms and corridors. It floats on clouds. Every picture sucks me in. Makes me feel like I have been there.

The last picture in the folder is of a modern-looking structure with a golden stepped pyramid coming out of the top. It's surrounded by a lush landscape that looks a lot like Earth.

• • •

MOK · Z · PED · U.A. · PATA

There is silence for a while as Mok and Z sit together.

U.A. has started inspecting every rock. She looks deep into them for something and sets certain ones into certain groups.

Ped gets up and touches the white cliff. He stares at the rock and then looks at the growing blue crack. Expecting.

Pata just lies there and stares.

Mok and Z look blankly at the white cliffs. Lost in a trance… Both far from here. Each being shown a world of their own.

Z comes out of her trance for a moment.

Z: "I don't want to lose this."

Mok continues to stare off into the haze.

Mok: "Lose what?"

Z: "Whatever this is. Whatever we've found in this place… It's like it shouldn't exist."

Mok: "What do you mean?"

Z: "After everything we got used to on Earth. The loss... The war... The way it felt to live on the ship. The way it felt to eat the same flavorless food every day. To never feel safe or comfortable... Or happy."

Mok: "This is better."

Z: "It's peaceful... The movement behind everything that's happening makes me feel calm."

The air is filled with tiny pops, a slow hiss, and the pulsing sound of waves as the blue line steadily grows bigger and Z drifts back into her trance.

22

SHAN

I was a research scientist before the invasion. I worked with cells and DNA and RNA. I worked to understand where life came from.

What told DNA to be? How did this DNA blueprint get made? How did a cell know it was an individual yet still a part of the whole? What was it that held all of this together?

What are the patterns that make you who you are? How did all these non-physical senses and synapses and beliefs and ideas come together to form something physical?

I studied sound and the effect it had on the physical body. I studied vibrational fields and how to speed up the growth of an organism by playing certain frequencies.

If I had known then what they were using my research for… If I had known who I was working for…

I thought I was helping to advance our culture and our society. I thought I was doing work that would be used for some good.

But I also should have known I was living in a world of greed and manipulation and deceit. A world of humans.

Genetic research will always get out of hand.

• • •

MOK • Z • PED • U.A. • PATA

U.A. holds two rocks. One in each hand. Rubs both. Feels every little crack and bump. She has built a small group of white stone and white rock and white mud figures and begins to work on houses.

She sets down the rocks and turns to Z.

U.A.: "What's the last thing you remember?"

Z slowly turns her head to look at U.A.

Z: "From when?"

U.A.: "From before."

Z turns her head to look back up at the white haze.

Z: "I had just finished eating. Soy and rice. Soy sauce."

A slow smile starts to grow on Z's face.

Z: "I went looking for my daughter. I assumed she was playing somewhere with the other kids. She was born on the ship, so it was easier for her. I walked back to my bunk and then out onto the deck."

Z swallows and takes a deep breath. She slowly comes fully back to the present moment.

Z: "We had parked somewhere in the North Atlantic. I looked out over the water… Then…"

U.A.: "There was a bright flash and small pop in your ears?"

Z: "That's it…"

U.A.: "And now we're here."

The white haze from above has begun to slowly drift down, spreading out among us. It slowly pulls us further and further out of ourselves.

• • •

PED

Peace on Earth… It was a buzz phrase. A fad.

Only the ignorant believed it could happen.

If they prayed hard enough they could make people change overnight. The nirvana they couldn't find within themselves would automatically exist for everyone in the physical world.

There was never meant to be peace on Earth. Yet at the same time there always was. And always had been. And always will be.

I had created very peaceful places for myself. At home. With my family. That to me was peace on Earth.

But for the greater consciousness of the world and society, peace was a delusion.

How, as a race, could we learn peace if we didn't live in chaos? How could we know to be peaceful if we didn't know how to overcome greed and anger?

We were all moving as a whole while doing what we could as individuals to create our own peace on Earth.

23

PED

Everyone is intrigued and terrified by the unknown. I am intrigued and terrified of the unknown. A part of me screams to let go of fear and embrace it. Damn the consequences. At least I'm not sitting still.

But I know I won't move into the unknown willingly. So I'll need to be pushed. And when you're pushed you either land on your feet or crash on impact.

• • •

MOK · Z · PED · U.A. · PATA

Z calls out to Ped who is still touching the cliff face.

Z: "Tell us more about Venus."

Ped looks over to Z and then around the group.

What is happening to all of us? We all look like we are lost in a daze, each drifting in and out of inner experiences brought on by this world.

This place looks even more fuzzy. Less real. Like the energy from the growing blue is causing the atoms and particles to vibrate faster. Breaking everything apart.

Mok pulls himself back and organizes his thoughts.

Mok: "Yeah, I want to hear more about this man."

Ped, Z, and U.A. move in closer to Mok and sit down next to him. Pata shifts himself so he is sitting up.

Ped: "I think he was one of the leaders... I never met him. Only saw him in passing. He would come by the camp and check in on us. To see how we were coping with the new environment."

Mok: "What was the environment like?"

Ped: "Well... I remember hearing something about the Earth and how it was like a pressure cooker due to the way we lived with the sun's radiation. We were bombarded every day by it. We had gotten used to it so we didn't notice how it had altered our genetics and how it made us all more hostile."

Pata: "But that doesn't make any sense..."

We all look at Pata. We're happy to hear him speak.

Ped: "I know… It didn't to me at first either. But the lifestyle on Venus was a lot more peaceful. Much more natural. Even though we were closer to the sun, it was cooler. They had learned how to use the solar radiation…differently."

• • •

SHAN

I close the folder and walk back to the man sitting at the desk.

I hand him the folder.

Shan: "Why are you doing this?"

"Excuse me?"

Shan: "Why are you showing me these things?"

"I'm not showing you anything. These are your files. For your eyes only."

Shan: "Why?"

"I'm sorry. I don't understand. This is your record."

Shan: "What?"

"Here. Take this number. Walk to the end of the corridor. Turn right. There will be someone to help you."

He hands me another card with a different thirty-three-digit number on it.

I put it in my pocket and walk out of the room.

• • •

Z

When the tides stopped, most of the fish stopped migrating and spawning. They got disoriented. Didn't know where to go. Didn't have a trail to follow. Didn't have a direction. The driving force behind their life was gone.

Jellyfish just sank. They couldn't keep themselves afloat without the movement of the waves. People fished from the ships but the catch slowly dwindled. Eventually there were no more bites.

We hoped something down there found a place to go. Found a way to survive. Found a rhythm. If they did, we didn't see any sign of it on the surface.

Up here it was just day after day of clear, flat water. Up here every day was still.

24

Symbols hold no meaning. They're a trap.

You take something outside yourself and believe it signifies some great power or some entity that is bigger than you.

But really all symbols have the meaning we give them. The mind gives meaning and power to something that is meaningless and powerless. We create the context by which we enslave ourselves.

Now mostly all symbols just mean fear.

• • •

MOK • Z • PED • U.A. • PATA

Ped: "The people of Venus had built these massive crystalline structures at certain key parts of their planet. They magnetized these structures some kind of way—I think they used the rotation of the planet as a source of raw power, and used the crystal structures as frequency generators that created a grid around the entire planet.

"Apparently it brought stability. There were no earthquakes or hurricanes or tornados. The grid neutralized the energy from the sun.

"I got the idea that it was similar to the wireless electric grid we had on Earth, but positive instead of negative. It was in balance with the natural vibrations of the planet instead of in discord. Our systems put out vibrations of destruction. Theirs put out vibrations of creation and harmony."

• • •

MOK

There were a huge number of deaths after the first invasion, but soon everyone went into hiding as best they could.

The surface turned into a wasteland of moon troops trying to break into the underground bunkers to get to the governments, and the governments doing everything they could to stop them.

They tried to keep the fighting contained in certain areas and take back land and keep up with the number of troops the moon people were sending down… But their technology was too advanced.

Everything the governments could think to do the moon people had an answer for.

The governments put most of their resources into making a clone army of cold-blooded soldiers. They would make new vibration-resistant armor, but the scientists on the moon would find the frequency to counter the vibrational structure of the armor. The governments would be back to square one.

The moon people killed off the clones as fast as the labs could make them.

And the regular soldiers like me just did the best they could to stay alive.

The good news was that the moon people weren't very interested in what happened on the water. Once people made it onto their cruise ships they were left in relative peace. No one really understood why...

• • •

PED

Every generation has grand ideas about the future. Accomplishments. Inventions. Changes in economy. Innovations to be pioneered. An unexplored horizon of potential.

But we all seem to get locked into a current that's stronger than our dreams.

A society. Expectations. The limitations of both. The reality that things are a certain way.

The dreams of spaceships that run on water are shelved for a fight just to survive. Any hope to bring about change is met with a wall of resistance from the status quo. With a society, one step forward almost always warrants two steps back.

I don't believe there's an innocent party in any of this. Who lost control first? Who gave up first? Who just believed everything would be OK?

It's amazing the things that happen in a lifetime. All the things we find important. All the plans we make. All the jobs we do to busy ourselves and give our lives meaning.

All to be swept away by the hands of whatever...

Others? Fate? Karma? Belief systems and ideologies and laws we wish we could understand but are pawns of instead.

Deep down, I knew something was moving the pieces. And we were all willing.

25

MOK · Z · PED · U.A. · PATA

Ped: "I also learned that the people of Venus had a part in the war. They were allies with the people of the moon. There was a group that fled Earth and landed on Venus after The Great War. They took all that technology, built a new civilization, and left what became the humans of Earth in the Stone Age.

"I think they feel guilty. Like they were in some way responsible for the state we were left in. But that doesn't seem right to me… I do think they're here to help."

All of a sudden the popping starts to increase and draws our attention back to the growing blue.

The being from Venus is coming back. We know what his presence feels like now.

His form takes shape out of the blue and we are drawn in closer. Instinctively we form a semicircle and watch this entity appear.

He looks more solid than before. We can see the strands of his white hair and the wrinkles in his blue robe.

He speaks with a deep warmth in his voice.

"Don't be afraid. Let your imagination wander. Then put it all together. Guide it."

We stare at him in awe, trying to take him in.

Mok breaks the silence.

Mok: "What are you trying to tell us?"

The being smiles.

"Look at the blue. See the lines of electricity. See the magnetic points. See the frequencies. Tell it what you want."

The being looks directly at U.A. He talks to all of us. But his words are meant for her.

U.A.: "I've never done anything like this before."

"Yes, you have."

U.A. closes her eyes.

All of a sudden the pace in the air picks up.

The white rock and white stone on the ground start to get brighter. Like millions of little lights. And the cliff walls start to glow and the light from within starts to bend out like light shining through a prism.

We can feel something start to gather.

It starts to rain. Like magic, rain falls from the endless white haze above us!

We can't help but laugh! None of us has felt rain for years.

Decades!

We run our hands through our hair. We look up and let the rain hit our faces. We open our mouths and let the water fall in. We spin around in circles. We dance. We jump. We feel joy for the first time in a very long time.

And in our excitement, we don't notice the man slowly disappear back into the blue.

• • •

MOK

We started hearing that the governments were losing. The moon people were too evolved.

The governments kept upgrading and insulating and strategizing, but it didn't take long for the moon people to figure it all out.

The hardest part for the moon soldiers was to root out the underground bunkers. I don't know how they managed it. Fighting through miles and miles of heavily guarded subterranean maze.

Our weapons were primitive relative to theirs, but they still must have suffered millions of casualties. It was like trying to root out an ant colony the size of the world.

It made sense that people started to believe the moon people were fighting for us. For the most part it seemed like they were…

26

SHAN

I walk down the hallway for what seems like forever. One door after another after another after another…

The building is beautiful. The veins of color in the giant marble columns move with me as I walk this endless stretch of hallway. Guiding my way.

But the beauty is defeated by the never-ending steps I take. One after the other.

There are hand-painted tiles on the floor. Every one unique. Each one has a different design. A different pattern. A different set of shapes. A different combination of colors. But eventually they all start to look the same.

I have memories of seeing these tiles before. Even though I know I haven't.

I am being prepared for the next one as I look at the one below my feet. They flow together and blend with the pulsing veins of color in the marble to create a larger pattern that becomes a disorienting haze.

I can no longer make out any of the details of this place. I stumble along, guided by the colors pulsing through the veins of this endless hallway.

I finally make it to the end of the corridor, but I don't see anywhere to turn...

Did I walk in the wrong direction?

There is only a door. Wood with a copper handle.

I turn the knob and feel the latch pull back.

I push the door open and step through.

I hear two voices before I see the beings behind them.

"They are a good group. They learn quickly."

"It is in their nature. To learn. To remember."

"Yes."

Two entities stand in a giant library around a small podium at the center. Maroon robes hang down to their feet. One has thick black hair and a short beard. The other has blond hair down to its shoulders.

Their attention is focused on a gathering of energy that forms on top of the podium. I don't think they notice me walk in.

An indescribable force begins to fill the room.

A ball of white light appears over the center of the podium. Gold and blue and white and orange beams of light appear around the upper edges of the room and begin to snake around the library.

The beams move in arcs toward the white mass of light at the center of the podium. They whip around and blend together, making a lightning storm of color.

The dark-haired being looks up at me.

"Come closer. It will be good for you to see this too."

• • •

Z

It never sat well with me that the technology to build the ships was readily available. But we weren't given it, or even "allowed to know it had existed," until we were facing extinction. And it wasn't the governments that gave it to us. They would have let us die.

Did the governments feel shame for withholding world-changing technology? Those things that would have prevented this war and advanced our race into a peaceful planetary force, one able to be a part of the great planets of the universe…

To wallow in fear and greed and stall the evolution of your own people…

To manipulate your race to the brink of extinction just to exploit a stranglehold for your own personal gain…

It is the work of evil. Plain and simple. Fear-driven, egomaniacal evil.

• • •

MOK • Z • PED • U.A. • PATA

After the rain stops we all settle back down into our own little worlds. The joy from the miracle of rain passes away. Reality descends again and we are left with more questions than answers.

Our little world is hazier than before. The white from above still drifts down. Getting denser and denser.

It's harder for us to see each other.

Mok speaks to U.A.

Mok: "How did you do it?"

U.A.: "I'm not really sure…"

Mok: "Can you do it again?"

U.A.: "I don't know… I can try…"

U.A. closes her eyes. We all wait but nothing happens.

Mok is uneasy. Unhappy. We can all feel it. But we don't know what to do.

Mok has something on his mind. He needs to speak but he doesn't know where to start. So he just starts.

Mok: "How do you get rid of images that will be burned into your mind forever?"

U.A. looks over at him with compassion in her eyes.

U.A.: "I think you have to rise above the mind. It's like a machine that keeps you locked into these repetitive processes and realities."

Z does her best to help.

Z: "Eventually it'll run you into the ground and destroy your physical body."

U.A.: "Exactly."

Mok paces now. Like a caged animal.

Mok: "Regrets and failures and sorrows and the treatment of others… The abuses we heap upon ourselves… We could be timeless but we are worn thin by our environment. Stripped of our guiding light by rhythms of the past.

"'Shed the unwanted skin' the voice inside me says… But how…? These images are burned into my mind forever, and I can't keep up or move forward with all of this…"

Z: "Maybe you should try to get some sleep."

Mok turns on Z. Hostile.

Mok: "I can't sleep… We're not allowed to sleep… Can any of us even sleep here…?"

Pata: "You'll sleep when you're dead…"

Mok stops pacing. He looks at Pata. And then at the ground. And back to Pata.

Mok: "But the dead don't sleep."

· · ·

PED

What is evolution anyway?

We have ideas that we can't use in the present moment. We have ideas about what we want the future to be. We have goals. We have dreams. We have hopes that are bigger than us and desires for things out of our control.

We don't know what will become of our life until we've had a chance to live. To let it all start to play out.

Things we took for granted take on completely different meaning. We have new advancements and breakthroughs that lead us to new perspectives.

What made us think we knew anything to begin with?

Our beliefs get broken down and we see life from a broader perspective. As our thoughts and ideas change, so do we.

We have to evolve to keep up.

27

MOK

The governments were always fighting each other, and it only got worse as the resources they were fighting over dwindled. From oil to fresh water to natural mineral deposits to chemicals… It never ended and people only became more and more divided.

A new enemy sprang up every day and got turned into the greatest threat to whatever by the media.

I can thank the moon people for finally ending the wars fought amongst ourselves over nonsense. Fear. Beliefs. Resources we could have all shared and sustained.

I think we all started to realize our common enemy, and it wasn't the moon people.

• • •

SHAN

The two beings stand around the podium as the small storm continues to rage in the center.

I move in close. Curiosity takes a hold.

Shan: "What are you doing?"

The one with black hair responds first.

"Building."

Shan: "What?"

"The future of your planet."

The being with blond hair turns its head and looks directly at me. Its eyes are pure white.

"It was time. The moon people were sent in to help in your physical world. We work a bit more behind the scenes."

Is that a smile on the face of the being? Is that meant to be a joke?

Shan: "Tell me more."

The blond one turns its attention back to the growing mass. The black-haired one starts to speak.

"The moon people were observing your race. Reading your energies, tracking your progress as a people.

"If you had evolved past this cycle of war and chaos, past the consciousness of the last Great War, they would not have invaded.

"But the karma from those times was still very active. The ruling and priestcraft still controlling the population. Controlling the physical freedoms and impeding spiritual growth with stories and fear.

"They were far more concerned with mental manipulation than with spiritual unfoldment."

The black-haired entity begins to slowly walk around the podium as the beams of color concentrate into a surging and pulsing storm of energy.

The blond one steps back and moves to stand next to me. It speaks.

"But the moon people also observed many good people. Humble and whole beings. Willing to move forward past these young ways. Able to love and evolve.

"So they moved in to rebalance your world.

"You and your group, and many others we are also working with, will be the future of your planet."

The black-haired one moves to stand at the north end of the podium and the blond one at the south. Both beings raise their hands above their heads in an arc and push downward.

The storm of energy begins to descend as the room around us shimmers.

I watch as they guide this energy down to the Earth where it explodes in waves of color to wrap around the entire planet. Almost like a new ozone layer.

Then it all disappears and I am falling into nothing.

• • •

Z

People. Massive amounts of people. So many, many people. You don't realize how many there are until you're all living on top of each other...

Cruise ships weren't meant to hold five thousand people. Much less fifteen thousand. That was the average. Some could hold more. I don't understand how they did it.

Communities were formed. People fell in love. Families started. You had to apply for a permit to have a child. They would look at the numbers lost and see if they could handle new life.

It had turned into just a formality. For a few years we lost more than we gained. But we loved having new life on the ships.

Humans can adapt to all kinds of lifestyles. In the end we all come together because we need each other. For love.... For compassion... For companionship... No matter the circumstances.

The harder the times the more people rely on each other to survive. Meaning fills each breath when you know how lucky you are to be taking it. There's more depth to the joy and the laughter.

When you can find joy within yourself even in the hardest times, then you know you're an old soul.

But no one can make it through life on their own. No one is good at everything.

• • •

MOK • Z • PED • U.A. • PATA

Mok slowly settles down.

We talk to help him focus on something else.

Mok: "How did you stop disease from spreading on the ships?"

Z: "We had a sick bay and labs for producing medicine and food… It was surprising… Most people didn't get sick.

"Once you lost the will to live there wasn't anything to do… People who didn't want to get better just let themselves die…

"But overall, people were healthy and the food from the labs was good. Everything you needed to survive."

Mok: "That doesn't sound so bad."

Z: "Well… You just had to be there…"

The world feels like it's breaking apart. Like the blue is shifting all of us into something different.

It's like we aren't made of the same stuff we were made of before.

28

SHAN

I appear in a pure white place with the soft, rhythmic sound of tiny bells and running water. I can see figures in the distance. Like moving shadows. Formless but in motion.

I try to walk but it doesn't feel like I'm moving anywhere. No objects for reference. No solid ground to stand on. No horizon to move toward.

Life is formless. Or it hasn't been pulled into form yet.

Before long the figures start to move closer.

I try to call out but the sound doesn't travel. It starts and ends in my mind.

The figures surround me and move closer.

I feel what I think is fear, but then something tells me I know better. So I stand still and let them approach.

When they are close enough to reach out and touch me, a voice speaks in my head.

"Welcome. We've been expecting you."

• • •

Z

The moon people were a strange group. They fought the war on Earth, but they didn't kill or harm people they didn't believe were guilty.

It was like the hands of the gods were coming to smite them for sins they didn't remember committing.

One time, a small group of moon people landed on my cruise ship. They had one of their holy men among them. A spiritual healer or monk or something…

They said not to resist, that none of us would be harmed. We didn't really have anything to fight back with anyway.

They walked through thousands of us. Scanning us. Allowing this holy man to scan our vibrational fields.

He stopped when he got to me.

He was very skinny. Big dark eyes. About seven feet tall.

There was some human in him. But mixed with what?

He looked me in the eyes.

"This one was there. But she is innocent. A light scientist. Interesting…"

He made what looked like a smile.

"We will see you again."

I called out to him as he walked away.

Z: "What do you mean? A light scientist? When will you see me again? What do you mean?!"

But he had already moved on through the people.

• • •

MOK • Z • PED • U.A. • PATA

Pata is anxious. We can all feel it. It means he's starting to come around.

Pata speaks out to us from across our little white cliff home.

Pata: "I worked on the moon before this happened… With the moon people. I have to tell someone. I can't help but feel like all of this is somehow my fault. I never could have guessed…"

We all move closer to him. Space seems to just collapse now. We don't walk over, we are kind of just there—next to him.

When we respond we all talk in unison through Z. Like we share the same thoughts and she is our voice.

Z: "It's OK to tell us."

Pata: "I was working for one of the government space exploration teams. I was just a tech. I would go up on missions and just make sure everything ran smoothly. Then we landed on the moon and they told us our mission was to continue building relations…"

Z: "Did you know there were people on the moon before that?"

Pata: "Yes… No… Not really… We were told there was intelligent life and races but they didn't prepare us for an entire civilization living in the moon. They were human… Just humans who evolved on the moon instead of Earth."

Z: "So then what?"

Pata: "So then I was stationed on the moon. I was put to work just doing regular maintenance on our ships coming and going. All normal.

"I made friends with some of the moon people. They were very kind… They always seemed to be talking over your head, but that's just the way they were. Lofty… Philosophical… I wasn't working with them so it was all casual. I didn't know what was going on."

Z: "What was going on?"

Pata: "Well, now I know they were studying us. We thought we were studying them… Helping them and vice versa… But they didn't need help…"

Z: "But they were always kind to you?"

Pata: "Always. Even when they invaded Earth. They took a few of us into a room, said they needed to talk. They told us everything…

"They told me I was good and my spirit was clean from the past and that I could live with them on the moon until it was time for me to go back to Earth. They killed the ones who weren't 'clean' I guess…"

Z: "I can't even imagine…"

Pata: "I was furious. But they were so kind and understanding… The feeling of your home being invaded… Your friends getting killed back on Earth… Everything that happened and I just had to sit there and play nice with the ones doing all of it…"

Silence.

Pata: "Eventually I calmed down. I was never a prisoner… Me and the ones who were left thought about trying to fight. But with what? We knew it would be useless… We had to ride it out…"

Z: "That all must have been…"

Pata: "It was life… Then one day they put us all in a room and pop. I'm here with you all. Terrified… All these things happening… Looking straight into the faces of the people I betrayed on Earth…"

29

SHAN

The shadow figures on the white plane form a crescent behind me and softly start to chant. A deep vibration starts to resonate through me and I feel the pulse of life quicken in my cells.

I feel like I am a part of bigger worlds. Our world and many others.

Like there is a vibrational connection to everyone that wraps around the globe.

It feels like being submerged in water. I can feel every ripple as the tide ebbs and flows. A network of movement connected by a shifting fabric of life.

I feel people move about. Busy in their lives. They go places. Live dreams no matter how big or small. Move toward loved ones or new jobs or to the thought of new opportunities.

It is the same all over the universes. Life buzzes in so many different ways and comes into being in so many different forms.

What is it that made the people of my planet believe we needed to be separated? By race? By religion? None of it makes any sense.

All life is a nomadic union of wanderers. From the beginning of our race we wandered the Earth, and before that our ancestors wandered the universes, and before that their ancestors wandered down from the higher planes in search of further expansion.

So what is it about our race that wanted to restrict? And limit? And control? Those are impossibilities. Useless efforts.

Our governments put strict travel bans on us and restricted our movements. We couldn't live anywhere other than the state and region we were born in. Walls were built to keep people out. And lock us in.

But living in fear is no life at all.

The shadow figures continue their chant at my back, and I ride the sound like a wave.

Slowly the white of this world begins to darken and I am surrounded by the night sky. I can see an expanse of stars flicker into existence before my eyes, like millions of lights being switched on.

The stars begin to shift in slow arcs across the sky to form a path that cuts straight through the black expanse.

...

z

I remember the day I made it onto my ship. I didn't know how I should feel...

Was this supposed to make me feel happy? Relieved? At ease? Like I had a purpose again? Like surviving was better than not?

My husband and I had migrated into the Alps and were living in one of the many communities of people who were trying to hide in the mountains. We were all still mostly living off scavenged food from before the invasion, but people talked about trying to grow food.

But then the government men showed up and descended near our community in cylinder-shaped vessels. The ships hovered like giant columns holding up the sky, and a platform descended from the bottom of one ship. Two soldiers in dark-brown combat uniforms were lowered down and spoke to us through speakers in their helmets. They said the area was no longer safe and we had to move or be killed.

The governments were quarantining the area because they believed it contained a large number of time tunnels used by the moon people. That didn't make sense to me. We hadn't seen any moon people.

We believed the governments just wanted us off the land. It was going to be turned into a war zone and they wanted us gone.

We were told to go south until the land ran out. My husband had started getting sick a week or so before we started our walk to the water. At first we thought it was nothing. Everyone coughed or ached or had headaches from not enough water or not enough nutrition.

But one night he got a fever and started shaking and the next morning he was dead. I can't explain it. There was nothing I could do.

The reality of death is a constant companion. It's nothing new. You get used to it.

But you never get used to watching someone fight to survive with all they have and losing anyway.

You never get used to seeing the will to survive leave.

There were two ships waiting for us. There wasn't enough room for everyone.

• • •

MOK • Z • PED • U.A. • PATA

The energy from the blue dominates this place. The white haze drifts farther down, continues its slow, invasive attack on our senses.

We know we are all here together, but we can't make each other out anymore. It all starts to become a white void.

It helps us to talk. It helps to have something to focus on.

Z: "Tell us more about life on the moon."

Pata: "There wasn't a lot to do... I was pretty much quarantined with a small group. A lot like here...

"But I could move around our little neighborhood. I went out to dinner with friends a couple times a week. They had little restaurants set up for us. We all had our own little houses. We weren't allowed to travel outside of our little town. It was a refugee town really. I think they built it just for us. It felt like we were outside... on the surface... But I knew we were somewhere inside the moon.

"Moon people would visit us every once in a while to check in... Let us know everything was OK... Bring us more supplies.

"The truth is, I was terrified... The whole time I was in the moon... I was never a prisoner but I was never free either. I guess it wasn't much different from life on Earth really..."

Z: "Did the moon people have a name?"

Pata: "What do you mean?"

Z: "Did they have a name for their race? Or did they call themselves Moon People?"

Pata: "They referred to themselves as humans."

30

SHAN

The chant begins to die down as the shadow beings slowly fade into nothing. I start to walk the trail of stars laid out before me. It looks like it has been walked by many beings before me. Rutted and worn. Old and weathered. But it feels like I am the first one to ever walk it.

It feels new and alive. Vibrant and healthy. Like it reveals different things to each individual.

It is the most direct path to where I am going. It is the most direct path to the center of our universe.

How had this trail come to be?

Who had first forged this path? Was it made by someone coming down from above?

Or by countless generations of trial and error by those going up?

My head spins with questions as I continue to walk this path across the night sky.

The path begins to narrow and gently slope upward.

A white light grows in the distance. I move toward it as the trail narrows to a thin, tightrope beam of light.

I feel a force start to pull me in and I'm consumed by white.

• • •

MOK • Z • PED • U.A. • PATA

The air starts to swirl around us and the pops and cracks and sounds of the waves grow louder.

Our attention is drawn to the growing blue as two beings begin to emerge.

We shift closer to the figures as they emerge from the static blue.

We can feel the being from Venus who has visited us before. But we don't know this new presence.

The being from Venus comes into focus first.

Who is this new entity with him? It is much taller. Much thinner. Its head is shaped like an egg.

They both settle into focus.

Like a rock hitting water, the second being sends a pulse of fear through the group.

One of the moon people takes full shape before us.

Is this all just one big trap?

Were we lured here into a false sense of comfort? Put here to share our stories so they can gather information on us?

Why have we been removed from our world and kept alive if only to be casualties of this war?

Does that even make any sense?

We still don't know what this place is.

The being from Venus speaks first.

"At the end of The Great War some of us went to Venus, others to the moon, and the rest were abandoned on Earth."

The moon man has a peaceful, stern presence about him. We are all still gripped with tension, but he seems familiar. We can all feel that this is the same being Z met on her ship. But each of us has the feeling we have met him before.

"The people left on Earth after The Great War were the ruling classes. The priestcraft. The ones who began the conflict and harbored dissent amongst their own people for personal gain. The moon people have been watching their development ever since."

The voice talking to us shifts. The moon man addresses us now.

"This new war was a karmic reprimand to the foolish ego of humanity. Although the physical bodies of millions have died, that which they are was in no way harmed. We are all the same when we rise above this world.

"Your physical bodies have been kept safe on Earth because you will need them in the near future. There are other groups like you. Learning. Being taught the ways of the lower, physical worlds. Millions of others are being prepared for new incarnations in new bodies. Some on Earth. Some not.

"The physical worlds are hard, and although it may seem that all is in chaos, that does not mean this is so. It is as it has been created by all of you.

"This war was meant to give you an opportunity to be free and start from the beginning again."

Before we have time to ask questions, an orange orb forms around both beings and pulls them back into the blue.

• • •

Z

Ever since the moon people visited my ship, I wondered when they would visit again. If they would visit.

I silently anticipated their return. I would let myself get excited about the new and untold possibilities these beings brought with them. But I didn't want to fool myself either. Become naive.

They never returned to the ship. But every day I felt like it was only a matter of time. Now I know I don't have to wait any longer.

The thought is making me feel like the lunacy is gone. Like the past is only an echo. Like the time of suffering is over. Something I'd just rather not think about.

Can we really look back on it now as a memory we'd rather not look back on and be happy it's over? Can we really move on?

I dare to dream.

31

z

I missed playing sports. Football mostly. I was never very good, but I liked the movement of it. Running back and forth. Kicking and jumping. It opened me up. Helped me let off stress.

All the things we thought we needed to be happy… Some of the happiest times were when I just ran around in a circle for twenty minutes.

We think we're so complex and complicated. We're not. We just forget to get out and run around.

I had a group on the ship that started to get a league going. It was a lot of fun putting the teams together and having the people of the ships come watch the games.

When we came across other ships we would tie up, and over time we started having tournaments. There was even a sense of pride that started to grow for our individual communities and players.

It all felt hopeful. And normal.

• • •

MOK • Z • PED • U.A. • PATA

The beings leave us feeling the same as before. Filled with more questions than answers.

Z addresses U.A.

Z: "Did the moon people ever come to visit you in the underground bunker?"

U.A.: "No… I didn't think they could get down to us… Or didn't know we were there… Or just weren't interested in us… But that doesn't feel true anymore. I had dreams I couldn't understand…"

Z: "What kind of dreams?"

U.A.: "I was in a place a lot like this… A white space… Usually alone… Sometimes I could sense a person or two next to me but I never saw anyone.

"There would be a moon person standing in front of me and we'd just look at each other. It never tried to talk or reach out.

"I never felt like I could move or talk… Not paralyzed… Just that moving or talking wasn't something I should be doing…"

Ped's voice slides into the conversation.

Ped: "Interesting…"

U.A.: "Why's that?"

Ped: "I remember having the same dream."

• • •

SHAN

I stand in a world of vibrant color.

People move in a chaotic rush of life around me.

I'm in a city filled with cars and trains and people on bikes and people walking and people talking and fighting and loving.

What is this place?

How did I get here?

Am I back on Earth?

This doesn't look anything like the Earth I remember.

I can't recognize the language they speak. But it also sounds familiar…

My head is spinning in circles trying to see everything I can. Trying to take it all in.

I feel a hand on my shoulder and turn around to see the man in the blue robe.

He stares directly into my eyes.

He touches my forehead and the world around us starts to move in fast forward.

The landscape starts to shift.

Buildings crumble and are rebuilt.

Nature overtakes what humans have built.

A forest grows and fills with animals.

Primitive people hunt with crude weapons.

And then crews come in and rebuild a new civilization in the same spot.

Consciousness threads from one present moment to the next, linking all existence by a constant cycle of evolution.

The flow of time...

The impermanence of the physical...

The flaws in believing that anything is timeless...

What do we hope to achieve in believing anything will last forever?

That's a terrible burden to put on ourselves.

A task that will never be completed. And will only destroy us in the process.

The man from Venus snaps his fingers.

Everything stops in a grey haze.

He walks away into nothing, and I am left alone as the shadow people return around me.

32

SHAN

Because of my work as a scientist before the invasion, I was put to work in the food labs. It was fascinating. Simple.

They had a library of elements and used frequencies and magnetic waves to speed up growth in compounds and nutrients that would sustain the physical body. It was almost like a sped-up version of evolution. Like a synthetic Garden of Eden.

Elements would be divided and multiplied by stimulating the cell growth with resonant frequencies. We could use cells from our own bodies, put them in new environments, and they would adapt and develop as something new depending on the frequency you ran through them.

Our entire food supply was genetically engineered. Some people made the argument we were cannibals. But I thought the whole thing was brilliant. It was like everything I had been working on before was realized here and now.

I still don't understand how the technology got there. Where it came from. How it made it onto the ships.

I asked the senior tech in the lab, but all she knew was that it was given to Nautico by an outside source. When she got to the ship, all that was there was an instruction manual.

We could only speculate.

• • •

MOK · Z · PED · U.A. · PATA

We feel it's best to keep talking. Like if we keep talking we won't all drift apart into nothing.

It feels like we speak into each other's minds now.

We can't see Z speak but we can hear her. We know she's there. It still feels like she speaks for all of us. Our questions focus on Mok.

Z: "What was the war on land like?"

Mok: "A lot of sitting and waiting and then a lot of running and screaming."

Z: "How did you end up there?"

Mok: "I got left behind on the land. My wife made it onto a boat but…"

Z: "I'm so sorry."

Mok: "I walked back to the area we had been removed from… It was set up as a military outpost… I walked right up to the gate and said I wanted to enlist."

Z: "What happened?"

Mok: "They brought me down into a bunker. I'm not sure how far down. Probably not very far. Took my clothes. Burned them. Gave me a uniform and a weapon. Stuck me up top on a guard post."

Z: "That's it? No training?"

Mok: "Nope. The first battle I was in… I was scared out of my mind. I just ran and hid. I didn't want to kill anyone."

Z: "No shame in that."

Mok: "No. It was the right thing to feel. That first battle… I was just crouched down. Hiding. Out of nowhere, one of the moon people was standing over me. Looking down at me.

"We just stared at each other. He could have killed me. I must have looked like a dumbfounded idiot. Mouth hanging open, locked up in fear. He didn't flinch. He just walked away.

"And then there was this feeling of peace that came over me. At that point I knew I wasn't going to kill anyone in this war. This wasn't my war."

Z: "And they didn't install any tech in you?"

Mok: "No… They gave us little tracking devices with digital screens that gave us the orders. They weren't interested in any of us. We weren't worth the time. They just told us where to go, gave us a vague mission. To them we were just bodies to throw out…"

Z: "We all did what we had to do…"

Mok: "That we did."

• • •

PED

People are never satisfied by the simple explanation. Life must be complex because we believe we are complex. We're not.

We're either dead or alive. All the labels and categories and classifications and diseases are just a distortion. A distraction from being dead or alive.

If you're alive, be alive. Don't come up with all these reasons for why you're going to be dead.

And if you're dead, be dead. Be happy you're above it all. Be happy you can see above the nonsense that comes with people fighting over what being alive means.

And for the advanced class, be both. Neither really exists anyway.

33

z

People were assigned to different parts of the ships. Some went to the engines. Others went to work on the renewable energy generators. Others went to the water treatment center. There was even an experimentation lab for new technology.

We set up a school where people learned how to work on certain parts of the ships. We even set up a little preschool. It was really just a place for the kids to meet and play. And for the adults to tell them stories and spend time together. Build a community.

It was pretty amazing. When personal wealth fell away. When no one was working just for themselves or for their bank accounts. When people knew they were working for the survival of the whole, all the greed fell away. It was replaced by purpose. Everyone did their job so we could keep life going. So we could survive.

People formed all kinds of groups. Groups that played cards. Games, new and old. Football. Music. A theatre group started performing plays in the main hall. A few bands started and would play songs they wrote and whatever songs they could remember. Some folks started making puppets and putting on puppet shows.

Eventually we all started to feel like we belonged. It was a moving city. A community at sea. And we almost forgot about the world outside of it.

• • •

MOK • Z • PED • U.A. • PATA

Z: "What was it like to fight next to the cold-blooded soldiers?"

Mok: "I didn't talk to them. I just kept my distance. All of us did."

Z: "What were they like?"

Mok: "I don't know… I never saw them sleep. They were usually wearing insulated heat suits made of a dense material resistant to vibration. As time went on they started to breed them so their bodies were denser too. Almost like flesh stone. They had low voices, lower than any human voice I'd heard, and their eyes were milky white.

"I was happy when the moon people would kill them. They weren't human… The moon people were more human."

Z: "I can only imagine."

Mok: "I wouldn't want to if I were you. I'm sickened by it... That just the idea of those things was even entertained. We should have known better."

Z: "The future will be different."

Mok: "Isn't that what every generation believes?"

Z: "Probably... But with all this...how could it not be?"

Silence.

Mok: "Yeah..."

Z: "We'll make it different."

Mok: "Or not..."

Z: "Then we'll just try again the next go round."

Mok: "And the one after that and the one after that and the one after that and the one after that..."

Z: "That's the spirit."

• • •

SHAN

The shadow figures lay me down... on an operating table? A bed? A sofa?

The shadow figures move over me.

It looks like they are motioning to certain parts of my body... My liver... My kidneys... My heart...

They take out a device that looks like…a wand? A shaped piece of glass? Like an arrow with a rounded tip?

An orange light begins to radiate from the device as they slowly move it closer to my chest.

The light shoots directly into my heart and I can feel my muscles start to loosen.

I can feel something grind… Or unlock. Gravel being dug out of the earth… Loosening of stone…

There's no real pain. Not as I know it.

But it feels like something is crawling out of my heart. Being pulled out by the orange light.

A new blood starts to beat through my veins.

It feels like my old life force is being eaten. Being burned away by a new wave of cells and DNA.

It changes my body from the inside out. Cleanses. Heals.

Then it all stops.

I can hear a rustling movement.

When I open my eyes the group stands over me.

Stunned.

34

What truths are sunken beneath the oceans? What depths are we not allowed to explore?

Truth reveals itself when the viewer is ready. What does it mean when your world is submerged and all the truths become inaccessible? What are we ready for then?

When the water starts to go down and the land is revealed, what will they find? What will they assume? What labels will they ascribe to us?

Will there even be a future generation? Will there be someone to walk over the fragments of what was? Will we have learned our lesson this time? Or will we have to repeat this class again?

When will this cycle end?

•••

MOK • Z • PED • SHAN • U.A. • PATA

And just like that, Shan is back and our white prison has substance again.

With his return it's like all the atoms and particles pull back together to form a physical world again.

We no longer speak into each other's minds. We have solid bodies. U.A. in yellow. Mok in his brown military uniform. Shan and Z in the patched rags of the ships. Ped in orange. And Pata in his grey jumpsuit.

The blue looks like it did when it first appeared. Slowly hissing and popping. Making a tear in the fabric of space and time. And the sound of the waves is somewhere out there. Just beyond our grasp.

Pata kneels down next to Shan. We don't know if he's angry or worried or happy to see him or scared.

Pata: "Where were you?! Where have you been?! You disappeared! How did you get back?! What happened?!"

Mok eases Pata away from Shan.

Shan is in a daze. He does his best to gather himself.

Shan: "Give me a minute. I'll start from the beginning…"

• • •

MOK • Z • PED • SHAN • U.A. • PATA

There's silence as we take in everything Shan has told us. The worlds he's seen. The experiences he's had.

Shan looks around at all of us. He looks peaceful. Happy. But stunned.

We all want him to have the answers. We all want there to be an easy moral to the story he has told.

Z: "There has to be a reason. A reason you're back. A reason…"

Shan: "I'm sorry… I don't know…"

Shan digs his hands into the white stone and white rock and white mud. He closes his fingers around the ground and picks up his hands to look at the rock and stone. He tightens his grip around the mud and stone and then opens his hands to let it fall back to the ground.

Z: "What are we supposed to do then?"

Pata: "If you say just wait…"

Shan: "There's nothing I can tell you…"

Z: "There has to be a reason it stopped for all of us. At the same time… It stopped for all of us, right? The experiences? This place feels real again."

We all stare at Shan and at each other and at the magnificent white world around us. A world that feels free and caged and alive and dead.

Pata: "Tell me about what you've seen."

Pata talks to all of us. He needs something to hold on to.

Pata: "I know we've all been having our own experiences. Shan wasn't the only one. Tell me what you've seen!"

Pata's desperation shocks us.

Ped answers first.

Ped: "I was just in a garden. Being shown different plants, different flowers. There wasn't much to it. I hadn't gone anywhere. I was just kind of spaced out. You all saw me. I could still talk. I was still here… But there too. I could look into the white cliffs and see the light from within take shape and form into a version of myself. I was philosophizing to myself about life and my thoughts and—"

Pata cuts him off.

Pata: "Were you by yourself?"

Ped: "No. I was with that being from Venus, the one we've all seen. He's very kind."

Pata: "Who's next?"

Z: "All of our experiences have been different."

Pata: "So someone tell me something! The reason for this has to be buried in there somewhere!"

We all look at Pata. He isn't angry. He's scared. I guess we're all scared...

Z: "I heard sounds... Bells...bees...violins... Pure frequencies. And every now and then the sounds would form patterns of light and would take shape... Mountains...rivers...people...entities... buildings...cities...planets... Nothing stayed for long. It was always shifting. It was like it was all happening in my mind and the longer we were here the more real that became, and then...Shan came back and it just stopped..."

Pata starts pacing back and forth. It only takes him twenty steps to get from one end of our prison to the other. He stops, quickly touches the white wall, turns, and walks to the other side.

Pata: "I don't know... I don't know... I don't know..."

Z: "Calm down!"

Pata: "You calm down!"

Mok: "You're not going to figure this out! Not like this..."

Shan: "Sit. Wait."

Pata looks at all of us. And then at the blue crack, which has settled down into a calm hum. A rhythmic pulse adding a depth to the sound of the waves.

Shan: "You know it won't be forever."

Silence.

• • •

SHAN

What can I say? What can I do? I have no control here. Do I? I just have to wait until something else happens.

I look at the blue crack in the world like it holds all the answers, but I don't know what questions I should be asking.

After everything that happened I should have so many questions. But I have no direction in my thoughts.

Should I walk into the blue again? Just to see? But I just can't. I don't have the strength. I can't throw myself out into the unknown again.

Not yet.

I assume I won't have to wait long. But I really don't know how long I'll have to wait.

It could all be over and this could be eternity.

An eternal cave of purification.

A rite by fire to burn off all the injustices and bonds of my life on Earth.

All the senseless acts of violence and abuse coming to the surface to be burned away here and now.

How long will it take to work through the karma I've earned over millions of lifetimes?

Maybe that's how long I'll have to wait.

35

z

The human consciousness has destruction built into it. The life cycles of humans, nations, and planets are all wrought with the drive to commit suicide. Whether it be immediate or slowly executed over a lifetime.

Everyone believes they need a fresh start. That they need to go somewhere new. That the Earth just isn't big enough.

But we're trapped in the consciousness of the time. And of those around us. Earth can be whatever we want. We don't need to discover a new one somewhere else.

There was an older man on the ship with me who would always say, "To choose death over life is a perversion of life itself." We had a lot to talk about. But that was what it all came back to.

We would meet for an hour or two every few days. Eventually others started to join. We started our own little discussion group.

I'd say it was philosophical but it was really more like therapy. Telling stories about the past. Sharing dreams. Thoughts about where the Earth was going. What life was like on the other ships. If we'd make it off the ships in our lifetime.

It's amazing how easily people can live and work together when there isn't someone trying to tell you how life should be.

• • •

MOK • Z • PED • SHAN • U.A. • PATA

We all need something from each other.

Shan starts to walk the perimeter of our white prison again. Sixty steps to walk the entire perimeter. He touches the white cliff face. Looks into the rock. Looks at the blue. Looks up into the white haze.

U.A. continues to build little figures out of the white rock and white stone and white mud.

Pata takes up rocking back and forth again. This time he sits up with his knees pulled into his chest.

Mok, Ped, and Z sit together and talk.

Mok: "What else can you tell us about Venus? What was life like?"

Ped: "It was hard to tell. They had us separated. Living in a little refugee community. I'm guessing a lot like it was on the moon."

Ped motions his head over to Pata, who rocks in sync with the sound of the waves.

Z: "Makes sense."

Ped: "Yeah. It was a little village in the woods. We had these little cabins that were built into the landscape. There was a type of deer. Or what seemed like deer. They had birds and fish.

"We weren't allowed to eat any of the animals. Something about how they were there to help maintain the balance of the planet for the people. They believed a planet without animals would cause everything to come unbalanced.

"They had a hierarchy. A society structure. But it wasn't like a government. It didn't seem like there were any laws or legislations. Nothing written down anyway. More like codes of moral conduct.

"There were places you could go if you were having trouble. Any kind of trouble. Health, finance, family, work. And they would help heal the issue with light therapy or frequency healing.

"Find a vibration behind your problem and clear it with a balancing vibration. Healing the non-physical root of a problem.

"People seemed happy."

• • •

Z

I was always so sure of myself. That I at least knew what was right for me. That I knew what I wanted and what I had to do to get it.

I don't want to keep feeling like I'm grasping at straws for purpose. Holding on to any little belief I can to feel important.

If I was meant to be doing something else, then why am I not doing it? Why am I here with these people?

My entire life has been spent searching for a feeling in the present moment that isn't the one I currently possess. An elusive happiness. Which I didn't know I had until it was gone.

So now I'm searching for it again in this present moment, not realizing that I already have it, so I can learn later that I don't have it anymore.

One cycle after the next after the next after the next… Until what?

Until I realize I've been grasping at straws this whole time.

36

None of the mental constructs of humanity have ever really meant anything. They've just been a sign of the times. A benchmark for a state of consciousness. Only the ego would think it's something timeless.

How would the aesthetic beliefs of humanity in the dark ages benefit the people of the twenty-fifth century?

The life we live doesn't make sense out of context. It's all just one big "you had to be there."

I'm finding it harder and harder to focus on my thoughts... All the things keeping me grounded... In control... All the things I need to keep telling myself... All of my beliefs...

Hmm…

Wait…

Well…

Shit.

• • •

MOK • Z • PED • SHAN • U.A. • PATA

Pata needs to speak. We can all feel his apprehension. We can still feel each other. So that's something.

A pressure grows from within as our nerves wear thin.

Why?

Why the relentless pulse of this place? Why this electric hum of the blue and the maddening hiss of the constant waves? Why the blinding white of this place?

Pata speaks.

Pata: "The whole time I was on the moon I just wanted off. The repetition was endless. Day after day. Everything provided. No drive. No chance to do anything different. No chance to explore. Now I'm here and I wouldn't mind going back."

We all glance at Pata. Uninterested.

Z: "What do you want me to tell you?"

Pata: "I don't know."

Z: "We're all in the same situation."

Pata: "I know…"

Z: "Your complaining doesn't help anything."

Pata: "I wasn't complaining… I was just talking."

Z: "Well stop talking."

Silence. The tension builds.

Z: "You know you didn't have it bad. We had to survive down there. We weren't just given an explanation and a place to be. Every day we had to fight and every day we didn't know if we would live. Can you imagine what it was like to give birth on one of those ships?"

Pata looks down at the white stone and white rock.

Pata: "I'm sorry. I didn't mean…"

Z: "I know what you meant."

The never-ending static hiss of the blue…

It was so peaceful before…

Now it sounds different.

• • •

SHAN

There are things in life so precious they must be given to no one or they will spoil. Secrets so pure that just the thought can taint them. Distort them.

People get their hands on everything. Nothing is sacred. Everything is misunderstood. Our world was perpetuated with anger because that was easier for people to feel.

It was more accepted to waste life away in technology that offered us nothing. A cold and lifeless thing we poured ourselves into. And it didn't care about us. But we loved it more than each other.

What does that say?

All of the precious things...all of the quiet truths...buried by the noise of society. It was near impossible to find anything of value anymore.

I tried to take my family out to dinner a couple times a week before all of this. So we could get out and spend time together. I like to think it worked in spite of all the distractions. Entertainment centers and video labs and portable devices...

I never let the children get any implants installed. I'm so glad I didn't. Those people had a lot of problems after the meds ran out. Humans were never meant to have computers in their bodies. It made them angrier. I don't know how people didn't see it. It made them so much less compassionate. As if that were possible. They lost the ability to see others as human.

They weren't human. I didn't see them as human... They willingly traded in their humanity for a tech upgrade.

They would hook little tubes into your veins and your blood would flow through a small generator to power whatever device you wanted installed. They called them blood motors.

These things could then be linked to your brain and nervous system and perform any body function.

New organs. Muscles. Nerves. Anything. Those were the basics.

You could put recording devices in. Put a plug on yourself for external devices. Virtual reality where you plugged in and the machine stimulated your nerves and senses. People could transfer memory data by plugging into each other.

Even sex had become artificial. People could plug directly into each other or connect over the internet and start running a program... You could add as many people to the group as you wanted and it all become one cyber orgy. It was marketed as a way to combat overpopulation or as a way to safely enjoy your natural urges.

Some people would stay in so long they would overstimulate their nervous system and become catatonic. They would still have life signs, but they would only react to stimulation from the tech. It was a death sentence really. No one had sympathy for the overstimulated and they just let them die. I agreed.

And I was the crazy one for not wanting any of it.

They needed to take meds to keep their bodies from rejecting the computers. To keep everything in balance.

When the med supply got cut off after the invasion and people were left to fend for themselves, their bodies tried to push the technology out. The pain seemed unbearable.

All of the ones who made it on our ship died within the first few months. I was surprised they made it that far.

Once the body died the computer would keep ticking away.

We threw them overboard. Just another non sequitur for the future to find at the bottom of the ocean.

37

MOK · Z · PED · SHAN · U.A. · PATA

U.A. has built a small group of white rock and white mud figures. She has set them all up like they were in a little village. Men, women, children, mothers, fathers, daughters.

She even built a couple small houses and domes.

U.A.: "It's all one giant cycle. We're stuck in the middle of it."

Z: "What do you mean?"

U.A.: "We think we have control. Think our time is special. But we're guided by emotions we can't control or understand and they just take the form of anger.

"When you're scared and cornered and can't process it you attack.

That was life. Everyone was scared. Filled with fears based on delusions and misconceptions."

Shan stops his endless walk around the perimeter and looks at U.A.

Shan: "So what are we supposed to do about it?"

U.A. looks up from her little white rock world at Shan.

U.A.: "I don't know... Stop being scared."

Pata: "We'll just continue to be stuck in the cycle."

Shan looks over at Pata and continues to walk.

• • •

SHAN

Everywhere people were trying to predict the future. Always with the future. Like the present moment wasn't good enough. Never good enough. Beating yourself up over the past and worrying yourself to death over the future.

No wonder we needed catastrophes. No wonder we needed pain. It got people out of their heads for a second. Got them to start living in the present moment.

Our Earth had become a psychological wasteland. People needed to do inhuman things to survive and spent all their time wired into technologies that created a life that wasn't human.

How can you be peaceful when everything around you says chaos is the only way?

Every member of the governments had the tech installed. They had all kinds of excuses as to why it was necessary. It didn't matter who you said you represented or what interests you held. No one seemed to represent the interest of a whole human.

And then they disappeared underground. Plugged into some computer and started controlling weapons systems with their minds. It was a virtual reality war to them.

Even with everyone dying on the surface. The people giving the orders were underground, sending their dictates directly to the surface commanders who would distribute them to the soldiers.

What were we supposed to do with that?

For all we knew their bodies were going to rot in those chairs while an impulse from a brain kept alive told a missile to fire.

I think I need to start getting over all this. I have to let it go.

Right…?

What do I have to gain from harping on all these things?

Over and over again…

What's the point of all this if not to move on?

Life was different on the ships. That way of life was better. It was a step in the right direction. As odd as it sounds, it was a step toward humanity.

Time waiting in this place is worse. It's worse than the ships.

It's worse than the government rules and regulations and bureaucracy.

It's worse than being at the whim of the entities.

Please don't make me wait here. I can't stand the silence.

Please… Please come back for us.

• • •

MOK • Z • PED • SHAN • U.A. • PATA

Mok, Z, and Ped continue to sit together. Talking. Looking.

Z: "Maybe all life is just one giant cleansing. We're all stuck here in the unknown, realizing the bigger parts of ourselves are off somewhere else trying to figure it all out."

Mok and Ped look at Z. They both wish they had something to say. Something to help her. Something to make her feel better.

Z: "I wish I was tired. I wish I was hungry. I wish I was anything. Something to make me feel like…"

Silence.

Ped: "Feel like what?"

Z: "I don't know."

Z slowly stands up and walks over to the growing blue.

She puts her hand into it and watches as her flesh moves in waves all the way up her forearm.

It feels like a slow current of electricity flows through her blood. Into her heart. And through the rest of her body.

She removes her hand, walks back to Mok and Ped, and sits back down.

38

PED

I have a song stuck in my head that I can't stop singing from beginning to end. Over and over and over again. It's amazing.

When you have the time to be quiet, your mind will latch on to something and not let go. Out of fear? Out of desperation? Like silence will destroy it.

Terrified of hearing nothing. Terrified of doing nothing. Terrified of being inactive. It explores the depths of a melody from a song I haven't heard in years.

But it came right back as if I had heard it yesterday. Like it was the only thing I needed to survive. Like it was the only thing that had ever existed.

Am I remembering it correctly? The way the verse and chorus weave in and out of each other as the rhythm pulses in the background?

If I could choose, I would sit in silence with an empty mind. But I'm the one who won't let myself be. I'm the one who is a victim to my own inner madness.

In truth I am nothing. I have no thoughts or opinions on anything. I don't care about politics or controlling people or making money or gaining fame or importance or society.

All of it is a product of my own inner madness. Of my inability to be still. Be free. Be quiet.

This damn song repeats over and over in my mind and I don't know how to be still...

How do I be quiet?

How do I not drive myself mad?

• • •

MOK • Z • PED • SHAN • U.A. • PATA

Z is losing her sense of reality. Her foundation. We can all feel it. It's happening to all of us. But she needs something and we don't know what.

Ped: "Some things are hard to make sense of. Why things happen. The reasons for..."

Mok: "Anything."

Ped: "Yeah."

Z: "Is that supposed to make me feel better?"

Ped: "I don't know."

Z: "Does it make you feel better?"

Ped: "No."

Z: "When I was living on the ship, my daughter would always make me feel better. Give me a reason to keep waking up."

Ped: "I understand."

Z: "But now… Where's my reason? I can't live for myself. I can't survive without something."

Ped: "This isn't the end of it. You've heard everything we've been told. You've had your experiences."

Z: "So we go back to Earth. Then what? What's the good in that?! Everything in chaos?! All my family dead?!"

Ped: "Maybe that's not the point?"

Z: "Then what is the point?! How many times do we have to start over with nothing?!"

Ped: "I don't know…"

Silence. The static from the blue crack has intensified. Hissing and snapping. An unrelenting torture for the senses. Like it wants something from us. And it isn't going to stop until it gets it.

Ped: "I'm sorry I don't know…"

• • •

PED

Stillness is the language of God. Is that why I can't be still? I haven't learned to speak the language yet?

There are no interpretations. No language stillness can be translated into. I have to go to it. It will never come to me.

I have to catch it as it quickly passes. Precious moments. No one can teach it to me. I gather it slowly over years and decades and lifetimes. Learn my own version. Speak it to myself.

But I can only recognize it in others. Once seen, what is there to say?

Nothing.

So I smile and appreciate the moment I caught it before it passed.

39

z

Everyone thinks the rules don't apply to them. Like they're special. They can get away with anything and life will just pass them over when it's collecting its hard dues and petty taxes.

But the farther down the road you go, the stricter the rules get. The less room for error you have. The risks get greater, and more and more people rely on you to know what you're talking about.

You can't play games anymore and just expect everything will work out. You can't live your life as a victim. You can't expect someone to survive for you.

We all learn the hard way. It's the only way we learn. A trial by fire. Day after day.

If only we'd learned our lesson the first time. If only we didn't have to learn the hard way. If only we had paid attention. If only we hadn't thought we knew better.

What made us think we knew better? Isn't that what every generation thinks? That they know better? That they need to reinvent the wheel?

We push against everything because it's in our nature. It's too difficult to allow life to be. We have to think of new ways to control it, and then life adapts because it will never be controlled. And then all we have created is a world based on fear.

An entire civilization built on a false premise.

I really need to get out of here.

• • •

SHAN

The electric charge of the blue works its way through me. It makes my cells vibrate at a different rate. Changes the way my body processes the signals from my brain. Changes the source of the signals my brain receives.

Each of us is in our own version of torture. Tortured by the truths of what we are. What we have done. What we have to atone for here and now. Desperate and terrified by what we have to do. A ritual of purification to release all that isn't meant to be here anymore.

To be replaced by what? Nothing? Truth? Death? Life? A new fear? A new cycle of death and rebirth?

My brain says end this madness while my body says I have only begun to purge.

• • •

MOK • Z • PED • SHAN • U.A. • PATA

Shan continues to walk around the perimeter on his constant quest to try and find something in the white cliffs.

Pata sits with his back against the wall, head in his knees. He looks up when he senses Shan get closer.

Pata: "What are you looking for?"

Shan: "I don't know. What do you think I'm looking for?"

Pata: "How am I supposed to know that?! How long do you think we'll be here?!"

Shan: "How am I supposed to know that?"

Pata jumps up and screams in Shan's face.

Pata: "I don't even know how long we've been here! We haven't slept! We haven't eaten! There's no way to know! We could have been here for years already!"

Shan: "I don't know how much longer I can take this."

Pata grabs Shan by his shoulders and pulls him close.

Pata: "OK, then what?!"

Shan shouts back.

Shan: "I don't know! We just have to wait!"

Shan shoves Pata to the ground.

Pata whimpers.

Pata: "How am I supposed to do that?! How am I supposed to just sit here?!"

Shan: "Do you see any other option?"

Pata lies in a heap. Crying. Lost to himself.

Silence.

Shan: "I'm sorry, Pata. If I had anything else better to say then I'd say it."

We all look on.

The feeling inside when you have no choice but to do nothing.

When you can't help.

When you've been forced into inaction.

There's a lesson here somewhere.

Buried deeper than we're willing to dig.

There are some things we just can't let go of.

40

PED

People don't like to think we have created a world that has made us slaves. To jobs. To society. To culture. To religion. To money.

We don't like to think we have so much freedom we're allowed to choose slavery. And we did.

Freedom is too hard. It's easier to create servitude. It's in our nature. It's in our vibrational code. Our karma.

Maybe that's what these moon people are trying to teach us. To set us free from ourselves. They're fighting a much harder battle than I thought.

I have to get out of here…

This place is driving me insane.

I get up and run into the blue. The others watch me…

Startled.

The blue violently sucks me in like a vacuum and my vision goes black. My body slams to a halt and I get shot back out of the blue like I'm being fired from a cannon.

I skid across the stone. Rock and stone and mud crunch and grind beneath me and I come to rest in a battered heap.

• • •

MOK • Z • PED • SHAN • U.A. • PATA

U.A. looks up from her white stone and white rock and white mud village and talks to all of us.

U.A.: "I'm concerned…"

We all look over to her but Shan answers.

Shan: "Concerned about what?"

U.A. scans the group. She focuses on each of us individually for a time. Like she's looking for something.

U.A.: "The dreams I had…"

Her eyes rest on Ped.

Ped: "What about them?"

Ped is still shaken by his failed attempt to escape.

U.A.: "There is something I didn't tell you…"

Ped: "OK?"

Silence.

Ped: "What was it?"

Silence. U.A. reaches out and picks up one of her small white mud figures. Holds it in her hand. Looks at it closely.

U.A.: "It's probably not important… Just a little detail I never thought about."

Silence.

She turns the figure over and moves it to her other hand, then sets it down with the others.

U.A.: "When the moon man was here, with the other one from Venus, I could see something moving in his eyes. Like twisting lines of light, bending and looping in chaos."

Ped: "I don't understand…"

U.A. looks back at Ped.

U.A.: "He was trying to show me something."

Ped: "What?"

U.A.: "I don't know."

• • •

PED

What are you reducing me to? What are you forcing me to become?

The never-ending pull toward something that is always one step ahead.

For a moment I am ready for whatever it is I'm becoming. Then I realize I was never ready. And never will be.

My ego in the background churns with impatience. I want to move! I want to be rid of this place!

But now it's time for the little self to be set aside.

All the parts of me that want and fear so badly. The parts of me that always believed I was ready and deserved more but never wanted to put in the work.

I've snapped faster than a dried twig.

And as the bigger part of myself takes over, it shrugs its shoulders and says, "What's all the fuss about?"

It sits me down in a corner to stare at the wall.

41

MOK · Z · PED · SHAN · U.A. · PATA

We all look up as the blue starts to grow. The blue crack in the world gets brighter. Bigger. It pulls our attention. It knows we're desperate.

Something moves behind the bright blue ripple.

Something reaches through…

Arms of white light reach out.

Is this what happens next? Is our time here in exile finally over?

Slowly the arms of white light move toward us.

We are frozen in place with…

What?

Fear? No.

Captivation? Excitement? Relief?

The arms of white light begin to snake toward Pata.

Pata stares blankly ahead as this unknown force moves closer and closer to him. He sits with his knees pulled up into his chest and he slowly rocks himself back and forth.

He looks terrified. But for the first time he looks ready. For the first time he looks like he can face what is happening.

Slowly the arms of white wrap around him like vines.

Tangling…

Winding…

Pata meets eyes with Shan one last time before he disappears. They are the eyes of someone filled with fear, but capable of handling what comes next.

Then the white begins to fade and he's gone.

Shan gets an impulse and darts straight into the blue crack and disappears. A stupid impulse.

But he can't just keep walking in circles.

• • •

PED

I carry this change with me wherever I go.

Everything I will be. Everything I will do. Is already done. It's just waiting for me to be ready.

It makes no difference where I am in the worlds. I am always with myself.

There is no context. There is no framework. There is just movement.

Wave after wave after wave after wave…

We are pulled out and drawn in. We expand and contract.

And every day we learn more about what it means to be.

All people. All races. All living things. No context. No framework.

Just movement.

From one life to the next.

• • •

Z

The world was such a beautiful place.

Why had humans lost touch with their roles on this planet? Maybe they hadn't.

Maybe we just did what came naturally and somehow that benefited the whole. We just didn't realize it.

We argued about how we were destroying this or that, when maybe we were too shortsighted to see we were pollinating. Turning up the Earth for a bounty in the future.

We believed we had risen above the food chain. But it wasn't so.

We lived in a constant battle to overcome death. A senseless struggle that only brought death upon us.

How can you be eternal when you're constantly focusing on your mortality?

The wars on the land taught us all different lessons.

The strongest will kill the most. The angriest will fight the hardest and longest. The manipulative will bend the will of others to theirs and believe they are right and in control. And the peaceful will do their best to be free among the chaos.

But even the majority of the peaceful, try as they might, will fall victim to the traps and angers of the mind and begin to fight.

Just another lost soul trying to scream louder than the others.

42

SHAN

I wake up with a fever.

Where am I? Am I back on the ship? I don't remember falling asleep...

I can feel the slow churn of the engines and I can see someone moving quickly about.

Is that who I think it is...?

"Oh my god you're awake!"

Shan: "Is that you?"

"Of course it's me! Who else would it be?!"

Shan: "What happened?"

"We don't know… Are you OK? You just passed out and we've been trying to get you back."

I start to lose consciousness. Blacker and blacker…

"No, wait! Please! Stay awake!"

I am immediately thrown back out of the blue. All the air leaves my lungs on impact against the white rock and white stone and white mud.

I am back with the others.

• • •

PED

Wisdom in our world has nearly ceased to exist. Even the philosophers have discarded wisdom as having no unitary value.

Knowledge has locked them in the mental realms and they have discarded the most basic truth in the universes. Wisdom is the universal truth. It holds the consciousness of us all.

All is known when the mind is forgotten and you are no longer rationalizing with the little self.

I say good.

Some things are too precious, and if hands could grasp wisdom it would lose all its value.

The greatest truths will always elude the human mind.

43

MOK · Z · PED · SHAN · U.A.

We all expected Shan to come back, so it's no surprise when he flies out of the blue again.

U.A. barely looks up from her model village.

Shan struggles to catch his breath and then scrambles to his feet and hurries over to Mok, Z, and Ped in excitement.

Shan: "I saw them! I saw my family! They were on the ship! They were alive!"

That gets everyone's attention.

Ped: "What?"

Mok: "What do you mean?"

U.A.: "How?"

Z: "How is that possible!?"

Shan: "I don't know! I don't know!"

Z: "So what do we do now?"

Silence.

We all look at Shan expectantly. The joy leaves Shan's eyes. His cheeks drop as the smile leaves his face. He slowly looks to the ground. The realization that we're all back where we started settles in.

Shan knows he was close. Knows he saw his family. Knows it isn't over.

Life still exists and we aren't allowed to be a part of it yet.

We're again left with more questions than answers.

Shan walks back to the white cliff face and again begins his walk of the perimeter. Inspecting the rock. Looking for something.

But that isn't fair… We're not back where we started.

We're here now.

We have to keep telling ourselves that.

• • •

PED

How do these beings see us? When we look into the unknown we know nothing. These entities are the unknown.

They are us. They have forged this path we're walking now. They have been here. Lived what we are going through.

We must look like scared little children. Struggling so hard to hold on to something. Something they had to let go of long ago.

We're the ones struggling for life. They have seen the struggle already. Lived it. Removed themselves from it. They know better. They're here so we can learn.

We're just another class for them. A chaotic mass of hooligans needing a slap over the head and a stern, "Grow up!"

How can we live with the shame of what we've done? How can we be allowed to continue?

I can't stay here anymore. Please... Please, I have to leave...

• • •

MOK • Z • PED • SHAN • U.A.

Mok, Z, and Ped still sit together and stare blankly up at the white haze, or down at the white rock and white mud, or forward at the white cliffs, or at the steady pulse of the growing blue.

Mok: "I spent so much time sitting and waiting during the battles, not knowing what was going on around me. This isn't much different..."

Z: "What have your experiences been?"

Mok: "I don't really want to talk about it..."

Ped: "It might help…"

Silence.

Shan walks closer to them. The static hiss of the blue and the crunch of gravel as Shan trudges on his endless march are the only sounds.

Mok: "Memories… All memories. Vivid memories of people and battles. Friends. Family."

Silence.

Shan stops next to them and listens to Mok.

Mok: "But it was like I was being walked through them…by the moon man. He was explaining how every moment, how every person who died, everyone I had to leave behind…how it was planned out. He showed me the patterns behind why.

"He showed me the bonds everyone had in this lifetime and how it was all in order with the karma they had earned from their previous lifetimes. How our past lives were our auditions for the roles we play in this life. And how we'd all meet again after this go round, say good job, and start work on the next."

Silence.

Mok: "It was little consolation."

Shan: "And you were here the whole time?"

Mok looks up at Shan.

Mok: "Yes. Well... I was here but I wasn't."

Shan: "I understand."

Silence.

Z: "At least you got to see it all from a new perspective."

Mok: "It didn't make living it any easier."

44

MOK · Z · PED · SHAN · U.A.

The sound of the blue starts to get higher in pitch. It feels like our ears ring from the outside in. A frequency hits our eardrums and moves to the center of our heads.

U.A. looks up at the sound and stares at the growing crack in reality.

U.A.: "Where do you think they are? Morla and Pata?"

Shan looks over at U.A.

Shan: "I don't know…"

U.A.: "Back on Earth? Or somewhere else?"

Shan: "They could be anywhere, U.A. Where are we now? I don't know where I was. When they took me away...I was places I can't even..."

U.A.: "I can feel they're coming for me next."

Z speaks from where she sits.

Z: "Why do you say that?"

U.A. looks back down at her little village. It's grown in size. She's built some bigger buildings and many more figures. It looks more like a village now.

U.A.: "Something about the dreams... What I saw in the moon man's eyes..."

Z: "What do you think it means?"

U.A.: "The only thing I saw were those shapes... Those twisting lines of light in his eyes. They've been slowly growing out of the blue this whole time."

Shan: "What do you mean?"

U.A.: "None of you have been able to see it?"

Z: "See what?"

U.A. stands up and starts to motion all around her.

U.A.: "The lines... They've never stopped growing. Forming a grid. Moving in chaos to form something perfect. Slowly growing bigger..."

We all watch U.A. as she touches something only she can see in the air around her.

Z: "Is that why you were able to make it rain?"

U.A.: "I think so... I just told the lines what to do. They came together overhead and then..."

Z: "Rain."

U.A.: "Yes."

Out of nowhere, lines of light begin to form a grid around U.A. The rays are all different colors, growing brighter and brighter, getting tighter and tighter around her.

U.A.: "I'm not going to be here much longer. But I'll see you on Earth."

Shan: "What...? How...?"

She starts to scatter and break apart. The grid consumes her physical form.

She disappears into nothing.

We are left again.

• • •

SHAN

My son had fallen asleep with his entertainment center on and I couldn't tell if the sounds I was hearing were from his room or from real life.

It was like a waking dream. A nightmare brought out of fiction. Slammed into reality. Relentless and unapologetic.

For the first few moments I didn't register any of it as real. The sounds still existed somewhere else.

The explosion happened on the screen. Existing only in my subconscious, somewhere between asleep and awake. A virtual explosion. A virtual rumble as the earth erupted from the impact. A virtual—

I was flung out of bed and we rushed to see what was happening.

An earthquake? A tornado? It was all so immediate.

Life was peaceful just a moment before. And then there were tall beings in space suits appearing out of nowhere. Flashes of light and a continuing stream of invaders from the moon.

Weapons were fired. People vanished into nothing. Our emergency response defense systems started fighting back immediately.

It was like one of those nights when you fall asleep with the news on. The sounds of the broadcast underscore a dream so vivid it leaves you gasping for breath when you wake up. But the peaceful relief of knowing it was all a dream never came.

Everything that followed was typical. Running. Screaming. Hiding. Scrounging for food. Survival. Avoiding the fight at all costs.

And the days went by and we migrated from one place to the next. Always moving higher and higher until we moved lower and lower and found our ship. Always in motion.

But I can't correctly remember the moment it all began.

The first moment the Earth was invaded.

It still exists as a terrible dream. Just a violent show my son fell asleep watching on his entertainment center.

45

PED

It's the process of purification.

The repetition of a task. The ruts that form our life's patterns. Deeper and deeper until we can't climb out or change direction.

It's a constant state of re-chemicalization. A constant search for balance. Finding the middle way.

In the lower worlds all is unbalanced. But still in harmony.

When the mind is unbalanced, all life seems unbalanced. It isn't.

We live in a struggle to find truth.

Find a teacher. Find a path. Find a goal. Find a reason.

We live with the belief that someone else will be able to teach us what's right. Will be able to complete us.

That is a misconception.

The greatest teachers will give you the tools to learn for yourself.

• • •

Z

Remnants of thoughts… I remember having so many thoughts.

All kinds of ideas that would run wild. Back and forth…

I can't think of anything important.

I can't remember why I was upset.

I remember I was…

Oh.

That's right.

Oh well.

Four of us left.

Probably not much longer.

This place doesn't feel so bad anymore.

I can't even hear the blue or the sound of the waves.

What will become of us?

No matter.

I don't know anything. How could I expect to know anything about anyone?

The layers and layers and layers of someone go so much deeper than the ego's ability to pass judgment.

It won't be much longer now.

· · ·

MOK · Z · PED · SHAN

They say the meek will inherit the Earth. Who then will earn heaven?

Karma and reincarnation will keep those unable to rise above the passions of the mind locked here, trapped in what will seem like an endless cycle of purification for injustices done present moment to present moment...

Life to life...

Over a course of time so vast you won't be able to remember what you're atoning for anymore...

But eventually the time will come when you're no longer spiritually meek and the physical worlds hold no value beyond a beautiful place for the evolution of soul.

The rhythms of the lower worlds become known and you will no longer be the inheritor of flesh but the earner of spirit.

The world chose to forget...

And then to slowly remember…

And then to forget again.

It is the only way to truth and wisdom. It is the only way to find the one timeless truth.

We are a caravan of souls traveling through time, working through different bodies, in search of the one core truth.

Forgetting everything time and time again so we can relearn and hone in on the one thing that is never changing throughout all our spiritual lessons.

So what, then, does the existence of God mean?

Are we not all God?

Given the ultimate task of coming down here to this physical world to live finite lives of ungodliness so we can remember what we are by living the furthest reaches of what we are not?

What is God anyway, other than the creative life force manifesting in its own unique way in all of us?

It gets distorted through the mind and the emotions of a physical manifestation of non-physical frequencies.

We are God made denser and denser and denser until even God forgets it is God.

The ultimate case of amnesia…

But it's what you need in order to learn the cycles of positive and negative... To learn to use the negative as a seed for change... To create and desire more...

You are very naive gods...

To think you know anything.

Terribly immature gods.

46

SHAN

It's time to move on. All that can be thought has been thought. I've walked every inch of this place. Found every crack and looked into the white rock long enough to see everything it has to show me.

My time here is over. This white world is like the house I grew up in and these people were my siblings. But we've reached an age where we need to take responsibility for ourselves.

I walk toward the blue.

The eyes of the remaining members casually follow my movement. Almost uninterested…

The beings are waiting for me. I can feel it now. It's an instinct like an animal following the lines of migration laid down by its ancestors.

Now it's time for me to do my part.

The blue starts to pulse. Almost in excitement. In anticipation of an event.

Something new. Something necessary.

The blue wraps itself around me and pulls me in.

The group slowly fades away as the white cliffs blend into a blue haze. I'm suspended in blue.

And then…

Where am I?

Am I back on Earth?

How is this possible?

The moon man towers over me.

• • •

MOK · Z · PED

Ped: "Why are we the ones left?"

Z: "I don't know. I want to see my daughter again. I want to go back to the ship."

The air vibrates as the blue continues to pulse.

Mok: "I don't know what I want… I don't want to go back to that Earth. I don't want to see any more people die."

Ped stands up and walks over to the little city U.A. built. There's a swirling of energy in the white rocks and white stone and white mud, as if they're slowly being filled with life. Colors slowly move in the stone like blood pumping through a body.

Ped looks away and walks toward the blue.

It isn't settling back into its normal rhythm.

It's getting more chaotic.

Restless and growing.

Static pops bounce off each other as the energy grows.

Z: "I'm scared of what comes next."

Ped: "Me too."

Slowly everything begins to rumble like a bomb is being detonated slowly over hours…days…months…

The white stones and white rocks start to jump and bounce below our feet.

This shaking is like an earthquake. The buildings in U.A.'s little village start to crack and tumble. The figures fall apart. Before long it's all rubble.

An orange light starts to spread slowly out of the blue and move toward us.

Ped: "I've seen that color before. On Venus. It was the color inside all the buildings… All the walls were painted that color."

Mok: "What does that mean?"

Ped: "I don't know. Maybe they're taking us to Venus?"

The orange slowly grows and wraps itself around each of us.

Life fades to black.

47

The moon man stares at me for what seems like an eternity.

Eons.

Something moves behind his eyes. Like golden snakes gliding across an endless expanse of black. His eyes become the only thing I can see. They consume me. His voice snaps me back into the present moment.

"I needed to speak with you."

Shan: "How long have I been gone?"

"Ten minutes of your Earth time. Maybe less. Plus that little stunt you pulled. Do you know how difficult it was to go down there and get you back?"

Shan: "Why do you need me so badly?"

"Do not be stupid."

It isn't anger in his voice. It is worse. It is admonishment.

I am an infant being scolded by an eternal entity. I am a naive child being told to grow up and understand the greatest depths of truth.

"Look."

He moves his hands together and pulls them apart.

An image appears. It's a still frame. Or…is it moving?

An image of my family and me on the ship hovers between his hands. I see myself asleep while my wife and son bend over me. Desperate and filled with worry.

"This is real time on your planet. As we have said, Earth was not destroyed. It was just being prepared."

He drops his hands and the screen disappears.

Shan: "Prepared for what?"

"The next cycle. The wheels never stop turning. The ages never stop rolling into each other. The cycles of life never stop."

Shan: "What am I supposed to do when I get back?"

"You will have a purpose when you return to Earth. You will find your group over time. Use what you have learned. Work together."

Shan: "Will I see you again?"

"No. You will not need me. Do not worry. It is all a game anyway."

Shan: "What do you mean?"

"Stop asking questions. I've shown you everything. Use it."

The moon man moves his hand toward me, touches my forehead with his thumb, and everything disappears.

• • •

PED

Humanity loves a frozen god image. As if a god would let itself be frozen in time.

Don't allow anyone to be made a martyr. It's the ego run mad.

Idolatry is forbidden because it locks your mind on one thing when God is fluid.

And the wrath you fear from making idols is the loss of truth.

It's to protect you from yourself.

Not from God.

• • •

MOK • Z • PED

A new world slowly takes shape around us as our vision returns. We stand in the middle of an empty field. Endless terrain in every direction. Brown earth below our feet, and blue, cloudless sky above our heads.

Our eyes fill with a natural light but there isn't a sun in the sky. Just endless, uninterrupted blue. It's like looking up into the ocean. You can see the steady color of the surface but you know there are endless depths suspended within.

The man from Venus stands in front of us. He looks solid. Like he's really here. Short white hair, dark eyes, and a blue robe. The man with the answers.

"You three are going back together."

Before we have a chance to answer, to question, to protest, the man in blue turns his back on us and begins to walk.

Toward what?

This expanse goes on forever. Brown and blue blend on the horizon like salt and fresh water. A swirling blur of two forces meeting.

We follow.

He keeps a steady pace. Always a little too fast for us to catch up. He never looks back.

He has become a beacon. The only thing that stands out against the brown and blue mirage we move toward. We must keep up. We must not get lost.

But get lost going where?

Endless terrain. Filled with potholes and rocks and bumps. We stumble at every step like babies learning to walk. Every little bump is an obstacle that could cause us to fall.

But the being walks straight. No missteps. It almost looks like he's gliding on top of the earth.

What is this place?

The wind starts to blow. Harder and harder.

A storm is rolling in. The blue sky darkens, threatens us with thunder, and sends cracks of lightning across its endless surface.

The being pulls farther and farther ahead. The horizon disappears and the world turns dark. Our guide becomes a blue light far in the distance.

We don't speak. We just keep walking.

Rain starts to fall. Hail. Our clothes soak through. The hail is a relentless assault slowly beating us down further. We have no energy left.

But we don't stop. We just walk.

And then the world starts to change. White flecks of snow start to drift across the brown earth. The raindrops slowly turn into fluffy white crystals of snow.

We are too tired to care. We begin to shiver as our clothes start to freeze. Our teeth chatter. Our ribs shake so hard we fear they may break. We walk huddled together to try to keep warm. It does little good.

Our guide is a faint blue dot we can barely see through the falling snow. But we know he's there.

The ground begins to turn to ice, and pressure ridges start to form around us. Frozen blue spikes arcing up into a black sky.

Our bodies yearn for the easy bumps of the field again. We slip across the ice. We fall to our knees. We help each other up to take a few more steps and fall again.

Warmth is gone. Our bodies are past the point of pain. How long have we been shivering? Shaking?

Our faces are frost bitten. Our fingers and toes are blue. How are we still walking?

The land slowly begins to slope upward. Up and up and up and up and up… Rocks appear below our feet.

A steady, rocky, icy grade leads to a high peak. A narrow path up the side of a mountain emerges. Our guide is gone but we know this is the trail we must follow. Every instinct screams that this is the way.

We climb over rocks and boulders. Jagged edges cut our cold fingers and the blood freezes as it leaves our bodies. Our feet blister and crack.

We trudge up and up and up…

We can no longer feel our bodies. We don't know how we are able to keep moving. There is no strength left in any of us.

Slowly the blue light of our guide appears ahead of us. At the top of the world.

And as we approach…

It all stops.

It all goes away. The mountain. The ice. The snow.

We're back in the field.

What is this? What is this heartless thing doing to us?!

He touches his hands together, and as he pulls them apart the magnetic blue lines appear. He steps into them and disappears.

The blue remains, vibrating in front of us.

Our bodies are warm. Our faces show no sign of frostbite. The gashes on our hands are nowhere to be found. The blisters and wounds on our feet are gone. Everything just a phantom pain.

We look at each other. And then at the portal in front of us.

We have no choice but to follow.

48

SHAN

When the world takes shape around me, I am in a forest.

Dense, green woods. Trees that reach up hundreds and hundreds of feet. I can't see the sky. The world is a shifting mass of different shades of green and brown.

There is no path. No obvious direction I should walk in.

The floor is covered with green moss.

What am I supposed to do here? Is this the end?

Is this the new Earth the moon people have created…and left me on?

How am I supposed to rebuild this?

I have no tools. Nothing to eat. No way to hunt. I don't know anything about the life that fills this place.

I sit down and run my fingers through the soft earth. I can feel something moving on my fingers like a million little bugs.

But when I look there's nothing.

I sit for what feels like ages. Staring into the trees. Looking at the dense, lush life that covers this place. I am captivated by the feel of the green grass and green moss and brown mud underneath all of it.

I haven't sat on the earth in so long. It's been years since I felt life below my feet. Holding me as I sit like a baby in a cradle. The vibrant life of this place nourishes me.

There are millions of words out there. Millions upon millions that people have created to define and describe. And yet none of them makes any sense when describing feeling. Or sound. Or love. Or…

There are no words to describe this world.

Words do not have any power of their own. They depend on context. Intention. Knowledge. Us.

The experiences throughout time have stayed the same. Only the interpretation of them has changed.

Life is an interpretation of the non-physical forces that move us through time. And words are an interpretation of life through the mind. Out of context they are meaningless.

I push myself up onto my feet. I walk over to a nearby tree and touch the rough bark. I drag my hand across its surface and smile when I see the brown stains and scratches it leaves on my palm.

The only thing I can think to do is start walking.

Find a place to build a shelter. Or find someone out there.

Maybe one of the others.

There must be a reason why I'm here. And I won't find it if I stand still.

So I start to walk.

49

MOK · Z · PED

We step out the other side of the blue and into a tiny house.

The walls are orange. A dark, warm orange that calms us.

The being in the blue robe sits at a small, circular table made of wood, waiting for us.

And the moon man sits next to him. His eyes... Like a window to the universe. Never still, movements of light that focus on each of us all at once.

There are three empty chairs around the table. The man in blue motions us to sit.

We slowly make our way over to the table, looking around at this tiny house we find ourselves in. The walls look to be made of some kind of mud. Orange mud? The floor is earth. A rich, dark soil that feels like a cushion.

We each take a chair and sit down.

The moon man speaks first.

"Humans destroyed the boundaries that once protected them. Creating technologies that stripped away their privacy and freedom. Willingly giving their affairs over for all to judge and look at like self-important cattle.

"Then they wondered why they had problems. Instead of sleeping they plugged themselves into computers and never gave themselves time to be peaceful. Or to be quiet. Or to rest. They did not eat without entertainment and they ate food meant for no living thing.

"They allowed themselves to be bombarded by propaganda. Every day your media would work you into a state of paranoia. Add the stress of daily life. How did any of you survive?

"Do you see why it was time for us to intervene? You needed help. As a race you had reached a point where you were not able to pull yourselves out of the hole you had dug.

"All of your businesses and religions were run with fear. Any message of truth in the major population was quickly suppressed or mocked or discredited. Ignorance was better for business.

"Any society with written laws and rules is a society of the lowest order. If you truly wish to be free, you must take responsibility for yourself.

"You three must remember this when you go back."

The being rises from his chair and stands before us like a statue. Imposing. Dominant. He is a wall. And his eyes have us mesmerized…

But we have to ask. Our voices sound like they come from far away… Pulled into the present moment from somewhere out of time.

Z: "Will I see my daughter again?"

Mok: "What about my wife? Will I get to see my wife again?"

Ped: "What about the others on Venus?"

The being in the blue rode responds.

"Your families will be with you eventually. They are having their own experiences. But you will find them on Earth. Some from Venus as well. You will see all before long. Focus on the here and now. After this you will be on your own."

• • •

MOK

There's no use trusting the promises of others. They're always looking out for their own interests.

An empty world is always filled with empty promises.

• • •

PED

This all must be fiction. Hallucinations. A fever dream. How can I believe any of this has been real?

I will wake up back on Earth and my mother and father will be alive and my journey to Venus will be the product of my overactive imagination.

But I know that's not true.

This fiction is real.

• • •

Z

We had destroyed the boundaries that once protected us.

50

SHAN

The spirit of all things fills this place. A life force flows from the non-physical down into every branch and leaf and bit of moss.

All life is a channel that spirit works through...

My thoughts drift as I walk for hours through the dense woods.

I walk for what feels like days. I don't know if I'm walking in circles. I try to scratch trees... Break branches... Build signs... But every mark starts to look like one I've made. Every configuration of sticks and broken branches looks like I made it.

But I can't remember doing it. It all seems off.

I can hear a scratching in the distance. It starts out of nowhere...

Or has it been there all along?

Claws scrape at bark… At stone… Digging into earth… Scratching and clawing… It becomes constant.

And slowly grows louder…

With every step I take…

My foot sinks into the green earth. The earth rises to remove any trace of my track.

The awful noise grows louder.

What is this new thing approaching me? This new terror in the dark?

Fear grows in me with each step.

I hardly notice that I start running. Scared out of my mind…

A mad dash to be rid of this beast. This awful, formless demon tracking me through the woods.

And then it stops. Everything stops.

As if I'd hit a wall, I'm frozen in place.

The noise is just the thought of an echo that rings in my mind.

I stand in a clearing at the edge of a large lake.

This is as good a place as any to build a shelter.

51

MOK · Z · PED

The beings leave us in the tiny house with the orange walls.

What do they expect us to do here?

What is so important about this place?

How long are we supposed to be here?

The house has a kitchen without much in it. Some pots and pans. A couple of cabinets with what looks like tea. A single gas burner. A sink. Some fruit and vegetables on the countertop.

Three bedrooms with three wooden beds. A bathroom. And the living room we were first in.

There's a garden outside with a wooden gate at the end of a path.

The house is built into a hill. A domed roof arcs to match the slope of the ground, making the house look like an extension of the earth.

We are surrounded by trees and bushes. Lush, green plants, some with red, white, and orange berries. Some with blue and pink flowers. When the wind blows, the leaves brush together and sound like running water.

There is no one else around that we can see.

Is this supposed to be our new home?

Ped: "This is exactly like the house I was living in on Venus. But this is more isolated… The first place was in a little village."

Mok: "So we're on Venus?"

Ped: "I think so…"

Mok: "So now what?"

Silence.

Z: "I'm going to take a shower. And a nap."

• • •

PED

We spend so much time thinking and trying to feel our way through life. Like any misstep will cause the whole thing to come crashing down.

How could that be?

Then we think of all the decisions we made. How we acted. How we treated people. And wonder how it all could have gone differently.

As if we could beat the cycles of time. Skip over to a different version of the future… If different decisions were made.

None of it is important now. We are where we are. Filled with hindsight but no foresight. Terrified to make a decision because of what we have learned from our past decisions.

So we sit and do nothing.

• • •

MOK

Wasting away the better part of your life in the slums of a town they won't let you leave.

Then you find someone who loves you for no reason you can un-understand. Who makes your life better. Who gives you purpose and meaning. Who gives you a reason to get yourself out of the life you hated.

Then war comes.

You try to stay positive and keep moving forward for the people you love, only to lose them one day because there wasn't enough room for one more.

Then in a life that isn't yours, you go to war and somehow end up in a house with three strangers on another planet…

• • •

Z

I didn't realize how much I missed the feeling of water on my skin, a bed to lie down in.

We take for granted all of the simple things in life. Water to drink. A place to sleep. A bathroom. Knowing that you're able to eat.

You don't realize how precious these things are until you don't have them.

I don't mind this little house.

It makes me feel like this is the way a home should be.

52

SHAN

Everyone needs to do what they're inspired to do in the present moment.

I have to keep telling myself that as I pull together sticks and twigs and grass for my shelter.

We are all creatures of habit, moving through life, doing the best we can to survive with the resources we have available. Conflicting balls of inspiration vying for territory and influence within the social consciousness of the time.

But what I'm beginning to understand is that we exist on all planes. All dimensions. Simultaneously. These planes come together to form the physical world.

When you leave the body, you are visiting a place that is a part of you. That makes all of us. But is not the whole.

We exist as the whole in the present moment.

When you realize this, you have no more need to travel outside yourself. Everywhere you could go, you already are.

It's a game. We all meet when it's over. Say, "Job well done!" and get ready for another round.

Today I'm inspired to build this shelter.

Tomorrow maybe it will be to try to catch fish.

After that to build a fire.

Then to explore outward beyond my little place of refuge. Back into the unknown to search for the beast that drove me here.

But now I need to gather moss.

Build a bed.

And finally get some sleep.

53

z

This is the first time I've had privacy in years. A small room with bare orange walls. A small, single bed with a wooden frame and a tiny wooden chair and wooden desk with nothing on it.

I don't remember the last time I was able to truly be alone. To live in the stillness that surrounds a place when there's no outside noises or people causing commotion.

Without the ceaseless pressure of the blue bearing down on me...

Without the endless feeling of movement that reverberated throughout that place...

The haunting presence of the entities...

The burden of being with the others and trying to keep balanced…

I sit on my little bed and look out of my window for what feels like hours. I stare out into the little garden with flowers and bushes unlike any I've seen before.

And I look out past that into the forest on the other side of the little yard. Filled with trees that reach up to the sky and life that I could only dream about before.

• • •

MOK

Hope whispers in my ear. Tells me I'm free now. That I'll see my family again soon. That I don't have to fight anymore. But hope is ignorant.

What makes me think any good can come of this?

Every day I woke up wishing for something better. Keeping hope alive.

But for what?

My own selfish viewpoint?

My own idea of how things should be?

I didn't have any idea how to get myself out of the world I was in. How to set myself free of the war. The violence. I had no control over the life I was living, so what makes me think I have any control now?

I know this being in blue will return. Tell us a story or a lesson. Expect us to listen and learn and hold his teaching in high respect.

So I'll stand there and I'll listen. I won't say a word.

But why should I believe any of this?

What proof do I have that this isn't just a convoluted version of the afterlife?

What proof do I have that this isn't what I've earned from the life I lived on Earth?

The whispers of hope… You can never trust the whispers of hope.

They're always just setting you up for disappointment.

• • •

PED

I walk out of our little house and to the edge of the yard. I rest my hand on the wooden gate and look out at the forest.

I slide the gate open and start walking a trail that leads into the woods.

It's well worn and narrow. Trees hang over the path, and branches make it hard to walk. But I continue to push forward.

I stumble over roots jutting up from the ground. They catch my feet with what seems like every step.

Rocks form steps as the trail starts to slowly dip down.

It gets steeper and rockier as the sound of water grows in the background. I can hardly see inches through the dense trees and have to focus not to slip on the rocks as I make my way down toward the sound of the water.

And then all of a sudden the forest opens up and the trail ends at a beach.

I walk out onto the white sand and see an ocean. Alive and pulsing. Rolling and Crashing. Filled with life.

Is this the ocean we could hear from our white cave?

I sit down on the sand, look out over the water, and slowly drift off to sleep.

54

SHAN

I wake to the sounds of birds chirping. My little hut is finished. I don't remember finishing it.

There's a little bird at the foot of the door leading inside. It looks at me side-eyed. Twitches and hops, chirps softly.

I look back in amazement.

Then it flies away.

• • •

Be watchful for the small miracles in everyday life. They can come in any form. Take any shape. You are always being guided by the forces of spirit. Working through you as a channel into the physical worlds.

Don't let the mind distort the signal.

• • •

I slide my feet onto the floor and sit up in my moss bed. I push myself up and walk outside.

The world is alive around me.

Wind slowly blows through the dense trees. Birds sing in the distance. Fish make small explosions on the lake's surface as they rise to strike from below.

If this is my new life… I think I can get used to it.

I take my clothes off and run toward the lake.

I loudly splash in and let myself float on top of the water.

The sun beats down onto my face while I float on my back.

The water cradles my body and I slowly fall asleep…

When I open my eyes again, the sun is setting and a scratching sound jars me out of my peaceful existence.

A dark figure stands on the shore.

55

PED

I wake up in my tiny bed in my tiny room in my orange house.

But… How?

I don't remember walking back from the ocean…

I sit up in bed and put my feet on the ground. The dark earth under my bare feet feels like home.

I run my toes over the tiny grains of mud. Feel the little bumps and knots of each particle.

I don't know how long I study the ground with my toes.

When I walk into the kitchen, I find that our friend in the blue robe waits at the table with the others.

"Good morning. I hope you are well. Here. Try some of this."

He offers me a small cup with no handle. It is filled with hot coffee or strong tea.

But really, it's nothing like either.

"When this war is over the moon will be put back in place. The waters will recede. The Earth will start to grow again. You will have a lot of work ahead of you.

"But remember this. Remember why it had to be done. Remember the moon people. When you are able to reach them again they will help you. But next time approach them with an open heart.

"You will be able to use the moon as a waypost for the rest of the universe.

"Tell others of these events. These things you have witnessed. These places you have been. It is the truth your people need to know."

Silence.

Mok: "Why?"

We all look to Mok.

Mok: "Why should we? How are we supposed to know any of this is real?"

Z and I look back and forth between Mok and the man from Venus.

The being stares straight at Mok and softly smiles.

He snaps his fingers and they both disappear.

• • •

MOK

There's a loud ringing in my ears and an unbearable pressure in my head.

I can't see anything… This damn ringing… I can't think…

My vision slowly starts to return.

The Earth is on fire around me.

But I can't feel the heat.

I stand where I had been when the bomb went off and the blue light came. I'm back on Earth. As it was before.

How is this possible?

The Earth is torn up and smoldering. Soldiers from the moon move across the land. Cleaning up debris. Collecting the bodies of their fellow soldiers to be burned. Turned into fertilizer.

How do I know that?

I look up into the sky and see the moon being moved back into place. A giant orb drifting closer and closer. It looks like it's propelled by an invisible hand slowly sliding it across a black surface.

And the water has already begun to recede. The tops of sunken trees dot the landscape.

It is true. But how…?

Everything we've been told. All our experiences. This is no after-life. This is real. I can't believe this is all real…

And then pressure in my head… And the ringing in my ears… It's unbearable…

And…

• • •

MOK

"Now do you believe me?"

I'm back at the house on Venus. Sitting at the table with the others like I'd never left.

I sit in awe, trying to make sense of what just happened as Ped and Z stare at me wide-eyed.

Mok: "Yes."

"Good. I will leave you all now. You will only hear from me once more. I suggest you make a plan."

The being gets up and walks out the door.

56

I am frozen with fear… Standing naked… Soaking wet… In front of a dark being.

I can't see anything but its outline.

The scratching and clawing and ripping sounds are a steady pulse that attack my body in waves from every direction. It feels like the sound is ripping my flesh from my bones. But there's no sign this thing has touched me.

It doesn't look or feel like any of the other beings I've seen before.

It slowly begins to approach. It glides into the water without making a ripple. No signs of physical movement as this black figure lurks closer.

The sounds of the ceaseless clawing start to focus... They come from deep within this dark creature and move in waves to hit me directly in the chest. Clawing through my flesh and bones to reach my heart.

It has no features. No form. It is darkness.

The awful sound wraps around me and pulls me through the water toward this living black hole. The darkness begins to seep into my body. It moves like liquid into my pores and into my ears and nose and mouth and eyes. I'm left blind, submerged in black with the endless sound of scratching and clawing and tearing.

• • •

The Earth holds the vibration of all the lives lived upon it.

If we want to grow along with the Earth, we must heal together. Let go of the patterns we have accumulated over millions of lifetimes and release those vibrations from the Earth.

Life is a cooperation. A balancing of energy.

Harmony cannot exist if we don't let go of the past. All life is equal as soul. And your soul cannot come through when you are consumed by hatred for others.

The Earth will heal itself when we allow it to heal.

We will heal ourselves when we allow ourselves to heal.

• • •

A crack like lightning cuts through the awful sounds of the black, and I stand in front of beings I can describe only as keepers of time.

Each one is a different color. Red, orange, yellow, pink, purple, green, blue. Featureless illuminations with the loose form of humans.

Their colors bleed and blend together at the edges of their outlines to form a wall of etheric light.

I try to speak but I have no control over my body. They drift through space and form a circle around me. The red one moves within inches of my face. I can see through its body of light as it hovers directly in front of me.

It has no face. No eyes. But I can feel it look deep into me. It tilts its head and—

A bolt of current moves up my spine and into my brain as all seven of these entities burst into my body. Every nerve screams. Fire pulses through my veins. It feels like lightning is cracking through every synapse in my brain.

And then a force starts to pull me up.

Faster and faster until it starts to feel like I'll be torn apart. I can feel the space between my atoms grow wider. My fingers and toes start to scatter into particles of gold swept away by the current pulling me.

The force intensifies and my arms and legs blow apart into millions of gold cells. My chest scatters apart and my head dissolves into the current around me.

I'm pulled and shifted like water locked into the ocean current. My atoms swirl and blend like a tidal pool until I'm pushed out into slower and calmer waters.

I can feel my atoms drift slowly back together. Their speed slows. They find form again. I can feel the weight of my body as I calmly drift on top of the water.

When I open my eyes, I'm standing in the lake and I can see the man in blue standing at the doorway of my hut.

57

MOK · Z · PED

After our friend in the blue robe leaves it starts to rain. A thunder-storm and a downpour. Lightning cracks light up the sky.

Another storm on top of the infinite number of storms that have racked planets throughout time. Another storm to wet the earth.

Another storm to make us hunker down and think about what's important.

· · ·

Z

There's a depth to the black when I close my eyes that's never been there before.

It used to be just black. The absence of light… Flat.

Nothing special.

But now when I close my eyes, I look into a black expanse.

There's an unexplored distance laid out right before me. Light moves through in waves like creatures moving in the dark.

Out of nowhere lines take shape and begin to move. They take the form of animals and people and buildings.

A man riding an elephant.

A woman walking out of an office.

A rabbit hopping through a field.

No substance. Just a grid to be filled in later.

The darkness when I close my eyes has come to life.

• • •

PED

I have the unshakable, lingering feeling of needing to be somewhere else. Doing something else.

But I have no idea what it is.

A feeling buried so far down, only the faintest glimpse trickles its way up into my conscious mind.

And even then, it goes against everything I know to be true.

But I can't shake it off… Only push it aside.

But it's something I will never be free from. Not entirely.

That there's something…

Out there in the vastness of the worlds…

Beyond all conceivable, rational belief…

Beyond what my mind has come into contact with in this life-time…

There's something out there that needs to be done, but I can't be-gin to fathom what it is.

• • •

MOK

I can no longer pretend this is a universe empty of intent.

It's not all accidental, mindless forces bouncing off of each other. Fearing what would happen if they stopped.

I'm tired of events unfolding before my eyes and feeling helpless.

Like I have no control over the course of my life.

But that's where the paradox lies, isn't it?

We will never see our true power until we learn we are powerless. We will never understand the depths of our knowledge until we realize we know nothing.

We will never know joy until we know pain.

58

The man in blue and I stare at each other for a short while. His dark eyes bore deep into me.

Locked in a moment…

Something I can't explain passing between us.

"Drink."

I am shaken out of the trance I was in.

Shan: "What?"

"You look thirsty. Drink."

I am thirsty.

I bend over and fill my hands with water from the lake.

I raise my cupped hands to my mouth and I can feel the water move down my throat, into my stomach, and then out through the rest of my body like it's filling my bloodstream.

"Follow me."

The being starts to walk down a path away from the hut and into the woods. I walk out of the water and follow him.

"Look. This is life. Beautiful. Simple. It doesn't require much."

We walk in silence for a while. I try to take in everything around me, notice things I hadn't seen before…

There are flowers and bugs and animals! Things I've only seen in books.

I feel like if I touch anything it will break apart.

I do my best to take it all in and keep up with the man in blue.

"All of this is made from two things. Light and sound. Look."

The being stops and slowly kneels down. He holds his hand over an orange flower. It begins to shift.

Ripples start to flow through it and it begins to dissipate. He waves his hand and the flower pulls back together.

"See? Everything is held together by waves. Light and sound. It is the order of these worlds. When there's no longer a need for that order, it will no longer be."

I nod. Pretending I understand.

"These are the basics. Thought and intention are the tools. Light and sound are the materials. Every cell has its own consciousness and all life works as an individual of the whole."

He continues to walk down the path.

I gather myself and follow.

• • •

Most people are born with just enough consciousness to make it through life.

Enough to be happy... To be sad... To be excited... To be disheartened... To fill their role.

Play out the karma they were meant to.

Step out for a moment at death and then come back for another round with another load of karma.

But everyone has a seed of truth buried deep within.

A seed that can grow into a life beyond the everyday.

A life where you can learn the power of soul.

It's no easy path.

It's a right earned only by those brave enough to break through the conventions of the time and see past the patterns of the lower worlds.

You will never move into the worlds of spirit if you don't first step off the path of endless reincarnations and onto the path of realization.

You will never move above these cycles if you don't have the strength to let go.

59

MOK · Z · PED

The rain continues to fall and the water begins to rise outside our tiny house.

We should be concerned…

But we aren't.

We should be talking… Making a plan…

But we aren't doing that either.

Instead we sit here.

Staring outside at the falling rain. Concerned only with the sound as it falls to the earth and the peace it brings.

We hardly notice when the water starts to make its way underneath the door, filling the rooms and rising around us.

What good is making a plan when we don't really know what we're planning for?

• • •

MOK

Like an ancient animal being hunted, there is an overpowering urge to be still and silent.

Hiding in the deep grass from a predator far superior.

If I move it will all come crashing down. Everything I've ever been.

But that doesn't sound right…

What have I worked for up to now?

Had I done anything? Had I gone anywhere? Had I accomplished anything?

If I get up and walk out of this house, nothing will come crashing down.

No god from beyond will scatter me into atoms. Like I failed a test so important I no longer deserve to keep living.

And yet I remain still and silent. As if any movement will shatter the precious stillness of this moment.

I can see the space between the rain.

I can see the space between the collecting drops of water rising around me.

The infinite stillness where we come alive.

• • •

Z

There is a static lump in my chest.

I can't remember when I first felt it… But there doesn't seem to be a time it wasn't there.

I can feel it pulling me down. Locking me into place.

But I can also feel it sending out waves… Up toward the base of my skull…through my brain…and out the top of my head.

Like a radio transmission being sent out into the universe.

It moves through my legs and through my arms, works its way to the tips of my fingers and toes.

I can feel it pulse out into the water rising around us.

Picking up signals, gathering information from the water and all that it is connected to, and sending them back to the source.

This uncomfortable static source… Buried in my chest.

• • •

PED

There will always be something standing in the way of our perfection. It will rage. It will bury us in anger. It will keep us locked in temples of flesh until we are able to shine a light on it.

Until we see it for what it is. A negative power doing its job to keep us locked into our struggle. Something to keep us in darkness, wishing for light.

What should I wish for in this present moment?

To not drown?

To stand?

To be somewhere else?

To be in a world that makes sense?

I can only act on the impulses sent down from somewhere… Somewhere I have to trust as myself.

How will I overcome the negative force if I don't listen to the voices guiding me along? As they always have been?

This is not black or white magic. This is not science. This is not religion. This is the middle path. The path of light and sound.

60

SHAN

"Read the vibration. Language is just a distortion. It gets in the way of true communication."

We continue to walk down this path through the woods. We walk through dense brush and across streams, through small patches of trees and over rocky terrain.

He continues to speak as we walk. Never looking back.

"All life can communicate through vibrations. You have missed everything if you do not see this."

We make our way out of some overhanging trees and stand on a beach at the edge of the ocean.

He stops and turns to look at me.

"You spend too much time studying the physical. You've completely overlooked where the physical comes from. Astral. Causal. Mental. Etheric. Spirit. And everything in between."

He points out over the water.

"Look."

My eyes scan the horizon and I watch the water gently break against the beach.

Shan: "What is this place?"

"That's the road back to Earth."

The man in blue puts his hand on my shoulder and I feel myself start to walk toward the water.

My body moves on impulse as I walk into the ocean. Step after step the water gets higher and higher until I let myself be consumed by the waves.

• • •

All life came down from the non-physical worlds.

The physical could not have existed unless a being on the astral wanted further expansion of consciousness and created it into existence.

As is true for the creation of all the planes in the lower worlds.

Moving down into denser and denser vibrations to learn more about the depths of creation and the limitless possibilities of soul.

When they found Earth they began a civilization there, as they did on many other planets, and helped create beings that were better suited for the environment.

Beings that could better handle the dense vibrations of Earth while still being channels for the non-physical.

But when you are so far from the core of truth, you forget what truth looks like.

So they fought and bickered and jockeyed for position until they destroyed their civilization and had to leave.

Soul is never concerned with its vessel's status in the physical worlds.

But their new race, humans, stayed on Earth, and continued to evolve in the rugged, harsh, and hostile world. Unable to remember or comprehend the truth behind how they came to be.

The saga of soul continues as we learn the truth of what we are by living what we are not.

61

MOK · Z · PED

The water continues to rise around us and we remain sitting in our little house.

I don't know why we don't feel the need to move...

Even as the water reaches our chests...

And then our necks...

And then rises above our heads.

It doesn't feel wrong to let the water fill our lungs.

To breathe in a new type of life force.

To let the water from this storm flow into our bodies and purify whatever it is inside us that is still too afraid to let go.

We have never felt so much purpose in sitting still.

Even as it all starts to slowly fade to black, we know this is all part of the plan.

So why fight it?

We let ourselves sit under the water as everything goes black.

• • •

Z

Soul was born out of the heart of creation when it wished for an expansion. When it wished to share the truth of consciousness with something created of itself.

When soul exploded out of this great consciousness it formed a massive ocean. Larger than any that has ever existed in the lower worlds.

But like any newborn, it was immature and rambunctious.

So it was sent into the lower worlds to live what it was not in order to learn what it was.

Thus began the cycles…

And evolutions…

And trials…

And errors…

And successes of life.

All of it part of the same consciousness. While also being an individual.

A cell in the body of the whole.

62

SHAN

I'm back in my bunk on the ship.

But I'm alone…

Where is everybody?

A voice speaks in my head.

I can see a glimpse of the man in blue.

But he isn't here…

He's just an image in my mind.

"Have you wondered why this has happened to you? Why you were with those people?"

Shan: "Yes."

"And what have you learned?"

Silence.

Shan: "I don't know…"

Silence.

"You won't hear from us again. But you won't need to. Remember us and the others. We have given you everything."

There's a pop in my ears and my family is standing over me.

63

MOK · Z · PED

The sound of rolling thunder and waves crashing with tremendous force…

Lightning cracks…

A pulsing wave of heat…

Made bearable only by the rain falling heavily on top of us.

But the world remains dark.

We can feel each other close by.

But we can't move or see…

Then a voice speaks in our heads through all the chaos.

The voice of our guide from Venus…

"You three have been returned together. There is a reason for this. Trust each other. Work together. You will find the others in time. Don't worry. It's all a game anyway."

There's a pop in our ears and suddenly we have control over our bodies.

We can feel our vision start to return.

We open our eyes…

The moon hangs in the sky and the Earth is on fire around us.

ABOUT THE AUTHOR

DANIEL AMEDEE is a writer and musician from New Orleans, LA. He tours and performs worldwide with his band LIGHT // SOUND. *Human World* is his first novel.

Learn more about Daniel at www.danielamedee.com, or reach out to him directly at danamedee@gmail.com.

If you're more of the social type, connect with Daniel on Facebook @DanielAmedeeAuthor.